Whiskey Kisses

3:AM Kisses Book 4

ADDISON MOORE

Edited by: Sarah Freese
Cover design by: Gaffey Media
Interior design and formatting by: Gaffey Media

Prologue

Izzy

When I was a girl I'd whisper my wishes and dreams into a jar, screw the lid on tight, and collect them all for someday. My world once had everything—powder blue skies, starry nights lit up like a pirate's treasure, and wide open meadows I'd run through while taking in vats of fresh North Carolina air. Then on a dime, the sun went dark, the stars faded to nothing, and I lacked the oxygen I needed to breathe. The night that my life changed forever, I opened the lid on that silly jar and let all of my wishes and dreams evaporate to nothing into the cold, cruel world I was abandoned in.

In retrospect, I can see the ominous pattern my life is mapping out. My world seems to fracture at least once a decade, and, seeing that I've just crested the horizon on twenty-seven, I'd say I'm overdue. I'm not a superstitious person by nature, but when you have a track record of misfortune it makes you uneasy enough to glance over your shoulder now and again just waiting for the other shoe to drop.

The first fracture came when I was just a child. My father left us when I was seven and my sister only two. He called me Little Bit, a play on Elizabeth, and I believed that was my true moniker to the point of correcting my teacher and classmates. My name was Little Bit because my father never lied. And it was so on that day he came to me with tears in his eyes and said he was leaving and never coming back. I stood stoic next to my mother, my sister dangling from her hip, and listened as he poured out instructions over me. Make sure Momma is never alone. Protect your little sister. And write me. Even though he said he would never get my letters—I did. I wrote feverishly. Every year I would designate a different color paper, different textures—one year they were all in the shape of a leaf. After a while I thought maybe when he came back I would string them out like party decorations and the house would be festive, dressed in the pastel sheets I bathed in tears. But he never came, the party never happened, and all of the letters remain entombed in a box where my father will never read them just as he said.

I wish I could say the next fracture happened as unexpectedly as the first, but this time all of the signs were laid out in front of me by way of wandering eyes, groping hands that belonged to the men my mother dragged home like pigeons she baited with a box trap. The night before my eighteenth birthday was the day the universe laid a bruise over my existence and burnt my world to cinders once again. The first fracture tore my heart in half. The second broke my spirit. I remember the last moment before I walked through that fire. The dance class I taught had just let out. The room cleared, and standing by the door was the brother of one of the girls. Holt Edwards had eyes so luminescent he could light up a dark alley at midnight as bright as a football stadium.

He tilted into me filled with all the adolescent angst you could ask for and said, "Izzy Sawyer, you are the most beautiful creature I have ever seen." He kicked the floor, and his shoe squeaked before he walked out of the room as if nothing happened. It was the last bit of sunshine in my world before I was forced to drink a bitter cup full of vinegar and bile, and to this day when I think of that horrible night, Holt's beautiful eyes still shine through the darkness like a distant ray of hope.

And now, here we are, all these years later on my bed with nothing but a bottle of whiskey splitting the difference. Holt Edwards looks at me expectantly—his eyes slit with wanting, his entire face glazed over with lust for me.

"Can I ask you a question?"

"Maybe." I feel it coming like an animal senses an earthquake rumbling, long before the tremor ever hits the surface.

Holt digs into me with those unearthly pale eyes. "What has you running scared?"

And there it is. I take another bitter hit from the bottle and let the fire race all the way down to my gut.

"So—you want all of my secrets on a platter." I blink a smile as the room starts to sway. "You tell me yours—I'll tell you mine." I've long since suspected Holt has been harboring his own issues.

Holt takes the bottle and indulges in one last swig before settling it between his legs. He looks up with a devilish grin, and suddenly I'm very damn thirsty for whiskey.

"Why do I feel like you're changing the subject?" I reach down and cradle the bottle with my fingers grazing over the blooming hardness in his jeans. "Hello there." I glance down as I move the whiskey to the nightstand.

"He can't quite hear you."

"Maybe I'd better bring my mouth a little closer." I run my tongue over my bottom lip, and the smile slopes right off his face. "Secrets?"

"How about we focus on the here and now?" He scoots over and pulls me onto his lap. His breath warms my neck with the strong scent of whiskey. When I was little, I would open that old bottle my mother keeps as a shrine and take in its scent. It always reminded me of fresh cut wood, of a forest, a man, but oddly never of my father.

Holt holds the scent of a country meadow, earthy and raw. His fingers dig into my flesh as he massages his way up my thighs. I roll my head and give a soft groan until it feels as if I'm falling right through him. Holt and I don't need liquor. We can get drunk simply off each other. Holt is the only high I'll ever need.

"I'm sort of liking the here and now." My heart thumps, wild and rabid, as it tries to break free from its cage. I reach up and run my fingers over his rough stubble. Holt is handsome as hell, kind, and I'm pretty certain he'd kill for me. He's my pot of gold, that's for sure. I wonder if he'd want to live in this room with me forever. How could I ever explain that those were the terms I promised my father—that I could never abandon my mother to the fate of being alone after she sacrificed so much for Laney and me.

"What's running through your mind?" He smears my lips with a juicy kiss.

"I'm thinking you should stay right here in this bed and never leave." I blow the words right over his lips. "You in?"

"I'm in." Holt lies over me, and my robe opens voluntarily.

"There's something I want to give you," I whisper as my heart fires in my chest like a gunshot.

"What's that?" He traces my lips examining me like this, naked and splayed beneath him.

"All of me."

1

Heart in a Blender

Izzy

Dear Dad,

Everything is going great. I'm on track to graduate, I'll be getting married in a few weeks to the man of my dreams, and I love where I work.

Actually, that's Laney's life. But don't worry about me. I'm pretty happy with Mom. And, most importantly, I've kept Laney safe just the way you told me. It cost a little more than I bargained for, but things that are worth it usually do.

Love,
~Iz

છાજ્ઝ

"Would you get a load of that tight ass?"

Jemma leans so far out of her seat I have to pull her back by the elbow before she does a face-plant onto the floor. She's waiting for her sister to arrive much like I am. Although I never look down on a minute I get to spend with my best friend since these moments are far and few between as of late. We're just killing time by staring at the aforementioned tight ass.

"Leave it to you to balance out equal rights by objectifying the male species."

"Oh, hon, I ain't objectifying." Jemma has held onto her country accent ever since she moved to North Carolina in the middle of junior high. It's one of the things I love about her. Jemma is not only fun as hell to listen to, but she comes fully equipped with a plethora of what I've grown to accept as Jemma-isms—slightly salted words of wisdom that are eerily on target. "If he didn't want all eyes on deck, he wouldn't dress that way." Point in case. Jemma is the worst offender when it comes to objectifying anyone with an extra appendage slung between their legs. She fluffs out her deep fried hair and plucks a cigarette from her purse simply out of habit. Jemma knows there's no smoking in the Black Bear—Holt Edwards and his tight ass have probably warned her enough in the past. She moans as he walks by. "He keeps strutting around in those bun-hugging jeans, and I keep noticing."

I sneak a glimpse at Holt with his tall, sturdy frame. He's built like a linebacker, muscular, but not overly so. He's got the same thick hair I remember and those illuminating eyes that look as though they have the ability to see right through your soul. He glances in our direction, and I'm quick to turn back to Jemma. A wave of heat floods over me at the thought of him heading this way. I've never understood how he has the power to make my heart flutter like a love struck schoolgirl. Whenever we meet, the air seems to thicken unnaturally. My body heats up ten degrees, and my fingertips tremble to touch him. He's gorgeous beyond belief—that should explain the blatant desire my body has to worship his. But Holt already has more than his fair share of devout parishioners willing to sacrifice daily at his king-size altar. He's a little younger than me, but obviously my hormones couldn't give a rat's ass if he were an embryo. I hate feeling helplessly attracted to someone, mostly because I hate feeling out of control.

He walks down to the far end of the bar, and I take the opportunity to further investigate Jemma's skintight theory.

"They're not bun-hugging." I tilt my head to better inspect our friendly bartender's rear assets. "They're loose and sort of low hanging. And, by the way, I'm pretty sure Ron wouldn't appreciate that." Ron is Jemma's latest spousal acquirement. At the ripe old age of twenty-seven, she's managed to amass three of them in rapid gunfire succession. She's two divorces up on me, and here I've yet to get out of the conjugal starting gate. Not that I'm looking to venture into that lawyer-laden not-so-great beyond. In fact, I'm pretty content right here in the singles stall with no desire to jump into the matrimonial spiral that seems to have swallowed up so many of my girlfriends. Jemma and I stopped juxtaposing our lives around the time she had baby number four with daddy number three.

Holt catches my eye again. He's lean and mean and full of enough testosterone to let everyone in a ten-mile radius know he's ready and willing to light any ripe coeds fire. But it's me he keeps stealing glances at—lingering those silver eyes over mine like a skin graft.

He heads in this direction, and I straighten.

Jemma's mouth opens to say something, and I covertly shake my head at her. Shit. Jemma is known to espouse all sorts of wild crap at the least opportune moments. Please God, let her pick another time to balance out the scales of tight-ass injustice.

"Hey, ladies." Holt leans over my shoulder and the entire left side of my body erupts into flames like dry brush in August. "Can I get you something? We've just put in a full lunch menu." He points to the laminated sheets that Jemma and I are currently resting our elbows on.

"Burger and fries. Throw on one of those fancy cocktails, too." Jemma wets her lips as her gaze drops to his crotch. "How about a Scantily Clad Cabana Boy for starters?"

"Never heard of it, but I can look it up."

"Oh, hon, you can make it any way you like." Jemma shakes the girls when she says it, and I avert my eyes for fear of having one of them poked out by an errant nipple.

"How about you?" Holt kneels beside me with his silver eyes harnessing the light and mastering its wayward beams. "How've you been, Izzy?" He breaks out a warm grin all for me, and my body melts right into the seat.

"I've been good. And you?"

"Same story, different day." He tweaks his brows, and my insides jump right along with them. "How about it? You up for inventing a new cocktail this afternoon?" He gives Jemma a quick wink at the dig.

"How about we keep it simple. Just a strawberry daiquiri for me. Make it a virgin." Much like myself. Virgin—Izzy Sawyer, they're interchangeable at this point. But just the reaction my body is having to Holt lets me know it might be time to rectify that. Maybe it is time to switch things up in my life.

That amber bottle my mother keeps in the kitchen flashes through my mind.

"You know—make it whiskey," I say. It was my father's favorite drink. My mother has kept his unfinished bottle of Jack Daniel's just above the stove for the last twenty years, and I've hailed it as a shrine ever since.

"From virgin to whiskey in a single bound. Whiskey it is. How do you want that?" Holt growls it out like a sexual command, and my entire body responds.

"Make it any way you like," I purr right back. I can't help flirting a little with him. His brand of perfection demands it.

"That's always a brave answer, sweetie." He gazes at me a moment too long, and I drink him in with his dark stubble peppering his cheeks, his intense glowing eyes—lips of crimson—and my stomach squeezes tight.

He takes off, and Jemma starts in on a series of spastic kicks under the table.

"Would you stop?" I retract my feet and scoot back an inch. "I'm going to bruise. And I have a class to teach in a few hours."

"He called you, *sweetie*." She presses her lips together, but a laugh bubbles through anyway. "Oh, hon, he just tapped you on the shoulder and told you to get in his bed." She shakes her head, pleased with her ability to connect the sexual dots—albeit incorrectly. "Ten bucks says you can have that shiny tight ass on a platter by midnight if you play your whiskey right."

"Please. I'm not plating him or anybody else up by midnight, and I don't plan on touching the whiskey." Maybe just enough to wet my lips.

"Knew it." Her eyes pull with sadness, an almost foreign emotion for Jem. "Does your daddy ever leave your mind?"

I slide down in my seat a few inches. Jemma Jackson has always had the uncanny ability to read me like a book—more like a picture book that shows the same heartbreaking scene on every single page.

"He does," I whisper. "But lately he's really been on my mind, and it makes me wonder what it means."

"I know exactly what it means." She touches her hand to mine. "It's time to get you to a good therapist. Trust me, hon, this is long overdue." She rakes her teeth over her bottom lip. "Make sure you get one of those touchy feely ones that know how to make you feel extra good when the session is through. We'll find you someone who's ready and willing to straighten you out a little."

"I know where this is going, and I don't need a sex therapist, Jem."

Holt pops up like an apparition. "I should hope not." His dimples dig in and—oh crap.

Turns out I don't need to worry about Jemma's wayward mouth. My own is quite capable of landing me in a steaming pile of humiliation.

He leans in, and his cologne washes over me like a heat wave at midnight. His cheek glides up one side as if all hell were about to break loose. And, judging by the way my thighs are quivering, it so is.

"Here you go." Holt sets a pair of matching amber drinks in front of us and the vanilla rich scent permeates my senses. It's a far cry from my usual catalog of virgin cocktails, and I'm pretty sure the only virgin in this scenario is me. It's nothing I'm shouting out over the rooftops, but it's something that's been swirling around my mind now that Jemma so subtly suggested I see a therapist who might be bribed into a one-night stand with the hope he'll *straighten me out a little.*

Holt lands a plate of burger and fries in front of Jem before directing his attention to me.

"Thank you." I give a weak smile. I've known Holt forever. His little sister, Annie, took private lessons at my mother's dance studio for years. Annie is one of the sweetest kids I've ever had the pleasure to teach. She was born completely deaf, but her determination to live a full life has put it in her heart that she can do anything she sets her mind to, and, for a while, that happened to be dance.

"How's Annie?" I drink him in. Holt is the all-American real deal—the perfect package for any princess in the market for a genuine prince charming. Six foot two, dirty blond hair, muscles for miles and, judging by that semi-lewd grin that knocks the girls off their feet, I'm guessing a quasi-dirty mind to boot.

"Annie is doing great. She's headed to Whitney Briggs in the fall. Her dorm is all set to go, so it's a done deal."

"Really?" I clutch my chest without meaning to. In my mind, Annie is still that lanky thirteen-year-old who wears coke-bottle glasses with a mouth full of braces. "College?" I swear I've inadvertently discovered how to fast forward time without meaning to. Sometimes it feels as though my whole life is riding on the tail of a shooting star—evaporating to nothing right before my eyes.

"Yup. Her move-in date is mid August. Bryson is still hanging around campus, so he can keep an extra eye on her." Bryson is Holt's fraternal twin. Their parents own a string of bars, and the Black Bear happens to be one of them.

"Hard to believe. Please tell her I said hi."

He glances toward the door and breaks out into his million-dollar smile. Aside from his eyes, and that decidedly perfect body, his big toothy grin is almost always guaranteed to melt a girl's panties. I should know. I speak from experience.

"Looks like you'll get to tell her yourself. She just walked in." He gives my shoulder a playful tweak and heads over to his sister who's currently being accosted by Bryson's other half, Baya.

"He touched you." Jemma gives that knowing look which is alarmingly always wrong.

"That's because he's comfortable with me."

"Oh, trust me, that boy is interested in making you *real* comfortable. Did you see the way he looked at you?" Her pale eyes pierce into mine with all kinds of inappropriate thoughts flickering through them. "He's interested in touching all of your comfort zones."

"Trust *me*, he's not interested. And would you leave my comfort zones out of this? See all those girls drooling over the bar?" I nod at a gaggle of coeds transfixed by Holt and his mixer-inspired magic tricks. "He can have any one of them—and, newsflash, he probably has."

"And what exactly is wrong with *you*?" Jemma kicks me under the table once again. "You've got ten times what those girls have."

"Would you stop using your stilettos as a gavel to prove your point? And for your information"—I glance back at Holt manning the bar while whipping the girls into an ethanol frenzy—"I'm no coed." I twist back and inspect Jemma for the first signs of crow's feet. Jemma's heavily drawn in eyes and disparaging choice of blue-red lip color really prove my point. "We're not on the same playing field as those girls. My mom always says—"

She holds up a hand quick to stop me. "No offense but your momma should be taken out back and shot on site for the welfare and safety of others. And then I should probably come back in and pistol whip you for believing a thing that woman has ever said."

Jemma isn't my mother's biggest fan. Although I doubt the working end of a rifle is in my mother's future either. They have a hostile relationship and still seem to get along better then she and I ever could.

"How is it that you call my mother 'momma' and yet want to hogtie her and riddle her body with bullets?"

"That's the beauty of who we are. Good old Bobbie and I understand each other because, deep down, inside we're the exact same person. We refuse to tell anything but the truth." My mother legally changed her name from Roberta to Bobbie when she was eighteen. Her father used to call her Bobbie, and she refused to answer to anything but. I guess we have that in common—our father's giving us pet names we prefer over the ones they originally gifted us with. Although if I called myself Little Bit, I wouldn't run the risk of being mistaken as a man like my mother so often is, I'd be mistaken for a less-than-amply-endowed pole dancer.

"The truth, huh?" I'm blinded momentarily by my mother and her stab-you-in-the-heart brand of candor. I love her to death, but she's honest as an assault rifle all day long. "Yeah, well, sometimes the truth feels a lot like a two-by-four."

Jemma slinks down in her seat, examining me with a slight look of pity. I know what she's thinking. About a decade ago I made the mistake of letting her in on my darkest hour. Sometimes I think the memory of it eats at her as much as it does me. But that's one truth Jemma will never espouse because I made it clear as the crystal meth her husband smokes that it's not her place to do so— it's mine. And I never will. Some things are best forgotten. And as soon as I can figure out how to forget it I'll be golden.

Jem picks at her food. "Rumor has it Greasy D is back in town—sniffing around old stomping grounds."

Greasy D—Don, is my mother's ex-fiancé who just so happened to remember our address last week and planted his drunk self on our couch.

"That he is." I blow out an exasperated breath because I'm not ready to go there. My mother has had a string of ex-boyfriends, husbands, significant other pretenders. You name the scoundrel, my mother has already teased him out from under a rock and brought him home. Most of my mother's suitors think they can make their way into my pants when she's not looking— one of them did. I shake the past out of my head easy as clearing an Etch A Sketch.

Jemma raps her knuckles over the table pulling me from my momentary trance. "Never mind all this bullshit. We need to get back to the topic at hand—you and Mr.

Comfortable." She snatches the pickle from her plate and holds its long, bulbous body up for display. "Now—I know his type—things are going to move quickly. He's going to flick his zipper and expect you to know what comes next. You're gonna want to pay careful attention, sweetie, because this is one pop quiz you're not going to want to fail." She plunges the poor defenseless pickled veggie into her mouth and proceeds to pull it in and out.

"Would you stop?" I do a quick sweep of the facility to see exactly how mortified I should be.

"No teeth," she barks over at me as if I were getting intimate with a cucumber myself.

"You can quit the tutorial. I won't be pleasuring vegetables anytime soon."

"You're not pleasuring anyone." She takes a hard bite. "Tell me this—you pleasing yourself?"

"I'm not doing this with you." I sink lower in my seat and clamp my hands over my ears.

"Come over some time. I've got a closet full of peckers that are guaranteed to make you blush for weeks. Of course, you'll have to get your own batteries. I wouldn't trust—"

"Jemma, I'm blushing *now*. Can we end this? I'm no more in the market for one of your closet peckers than I am for pickle tutorial. But, trust me, the next time I'm in a relationship with mildly-processed produce you'll be the first to know."

"No teeth." She bites the air. "One day you'll find yourself playing with Holt Edwards' pickle, and you'll remember this very conversation."

"God." I lean in hard. "You just said his name and the word pickle in the same sentence." I glance over at him still ten skanks deep as he shakes a martini mixer over his head. "Do you know people are able to hear their names at freakishly low decibels? He's going to think we're perverts, when we both know the only pervert around here is you."

"Guess I'll be his favorite." She smashes the butt of her cigarette into the table as if she were putting it out. "The things I could teach you if you only let me. Believe me, I've got a sexual IQ that would baffle the scientific community."

"In that case, you should consider donating your brain to science. Right now. *Go.*"

Jemma and I enter a standoff, just staring one another down with nothing but a headless pickle between us to pass judgment.

A pair of pale arms wave from the bar, catching my attention. Laney smiles like a loon as she heads this way. My heart warms at the sight of my sweet baby sis. She's been working here for almost a year, and, each time she talks about the place, she seems really happy as if she's wanted to do this all along. But, then, everything always works out for Laney. She and her longtime boyfriend, Ryder, are getting married in a few short months, thus the spastic text to meet her at the Black Bear this afternoon. I don't mind. It's actually quiet here today. It's officially June, so most of the people who live in this college town are gone for the summer.

"Bring Lila down to the studio." I tap my fingers over the table to garner Jemma's wandering attention. Every time Holt walks by, her eyes sway in his fitted-denim direction.

"Are you kidding? And reward the little shit? She turned the channel yesterday and forced her brothers to watch a horror movie."

"That's a new one for her." Lila is Jem's six-year-old daughter, and according to Jemma, she might be Satan's spawn. "And where were you while the kids were subject to teen vampires in love?"

"Napping. Believe it or not, I'm the only damn person in the house who appreciates a good snooze-fest in the middle of the afternoon. I'm telling you, this summer is going to be the death of me."

"Have they already handed out mother of the year?" I tease. "Because I think you're a front-runner."

"Damn straight I am."

Laney fast approaches with two girls in tow.

"Izzy!" Laney pulls me into a hug and her cute, perky friend, Baya, gives a shy wave from behind. Roxy Capwell, her soon to be sister-in-law is next to her. "You remember Baya and Roxy, right?"

"Of course, I remember Baya, and I'll never forget Roxy." I lean over and give a deep rocking hug to my once upon a dance student. When Roxy was coming to the studio she was a shy, sweet thing, and now she's a gorgeous-as-all-hell Goth girl who looks like she'd gut you for kicks if you smile the wrong way.

Roxy pulls back. "How's everything at the ELDS?"

I've pretty much taken over the Electric Lights Dance Studio from my mother.

"Great," I whisper, pulling away. Her eyes shine a deep shade of navy. Her pale skin acts as a dramatic backdrop for her dark hair with its cherry highlights. Roxy is a true beauty—heck, they all are. "And I never thanked you properly for throwing up on my favorite strappy heels a few months back. I cut myself out of them, by the way." And swore off strappy footwear for the rest of my natural days. Anytime you voluntarily place yourself in bondage to try and garner the attention of the opposite sex, it's not worth the effort. Then again, I'm never really after the attention of the opposite sex. That night happened to be another one of my sister's hair-brained attempts at finding me a horizontal dance partner. You would think there was a crisis situation-taking place in my jeans that only a male spare part could fully alleviate. I don't think Laney could ever understand the last thing I'm looking for is something quick and dirty. I've had enough unwanted physical attention to last a lifetime. But Laney doesn't know that either. There are some things a little sister shouldn't have to deal with. I've been protecting Laney for as long as I can remember, and I'm not going to stop now.

Holt's sister, Annie, comes over, and I pull an empty seat right next to mine. She offers the sweetest, strongest hug, and it's not until we pull away do I even see that she's all grown up and a beauty queen in her own right. Gone are the coke-bottle glasses and braces, traded for diamond cut eyes that rival her brother's, and a dazzling smile.

"Would you look at this?" I gasp at Laney. "We've got a bona fide supermodel among us." I look to Roxy and Baya. "All of you."

Annie gives a bashful smile and shakes her head refuting the idea. I can sign just enough to get by, but, for the most, part Annie is exceptionally good at reading lips.

"Two of my favorite students in one place." I take them in. "You guys should come back to the studio sometime. We're offering adult classes on the weekends."

They exchange glances, making it pretty clear they have better things to do than trip the lights on a Saturday.

"Well, I gotta fly." Jemma gives a quick glance around. "If you see my sister, tell the little brat I waited a solid fifteen. Ron is going to hack his head off if he has to sit on those kids another damn minute." She takes a few swigs of the whiskey concoction Holt was kind enough to bring and slaps me a high five before jetting out the door.

Laney shakes her head. "It's always a pleasure, Jem." She cuts her dark blue eyes to mine. Laney and I look nearly identical, but my hair is longer and darker, my eyes just a touch lighter than hers. "She stiff you with the bill again?" Laney doesn't wait for an answer. "Seriously, Iz? You need new friends. That girl has been trouble since you were fifteen."

"Thank you, Mom." I take a sip of my drink and feel the burn travel all the way down to my stomach. "Is that what you dragged me here to say?"

She gives a wry smile. "I dragged you here because I thought it would be nice to have my whole bridal party together at least once before the wedding."

Bridal party? I glance to Annie. That's strange, I never knew Laney and Annie were that close. Roxy is Ryder's sister so that makes sense.

"And"—she wiggles her shoulders—"we're having a sort of impromptu engagement party next Saturday night right here at the Black Bear." She slips Baya a secretive smile. "In fact, we'll be making a very special announcement, and I don't want any of you to miss it."

"So August 10th is the big day, huh?" I'm thrilled for my sister. There's nothing in this world I want more than for her to embrace that great happily ever after with Ryder. I love Laney with my whole heart. I would do anything to protect her. And I did vigilantly for years.

"That's the day." She grips Baya by the hand and giggles. "Anyway, it means the world to me that each of you is willing to be a part of my big moment. Ryder and I have decided we're paying for each of your dresses, and I'd like for you to pick out your own from the bridal shop in Jepson. Anything you want as long as it's black. We're going with that whole classic theme with clean lines." She wrinkles her nose at Baya. "Just something simple." She loses herself in a giggle fit once again, and Baya makes large eyes at her as if telling her to knock it off.

"Okay, we get it. You're happy." Roxy leans toward Baya and Laney. "But something else is going on. What is it?"

Roxy has a no-nonsense appeal about her. I've always appreciated that.

"Oh, just something." Baya waves to Bryson by the door. "I'd better go kiss my boss before I get fired." She trots over to her fiancé with her ponytail wagging, and, for a second, I think she's about to make-out with Holt because they look so much alike.

Marley, Jemma's younger sister, walks through the door, and I wave her over.

"I've gotta run myself," Laney says, getting up. "My shift started ten minutes ago. Just remember to get fitted by the end of the week, and don't change dress sizes before August."

Roxy scoots over. "Sorry about your shoes." Her face remains expressionless, and yet I know she means it. "I do miss the studio by the way. How about I gift Electric Lights two-dozen cupcakes, any flavor of your choosing. I'm a full-fledged baker now." She brims with pride.

"That is so awesome! I'm really proud of you for following your passion."

She glances up. "Speaking of passion." Roxy jumps to her feet and wraps her arms around a gorgeous dark-haired boy. "This is Cole. He stole the heart I never knew I had."

"Nice to meet you," I say. "And, for the record, I knew she had a heart. She used to stomp on it for fun back in her dance hall days."

"Nice to meet you, too." He grins down at me. "And I'll be the first to testify she has a heart the size of Texas."

"You found a good one. Okay, Rox, I'll take you up on those cupcakes. The ELDS is celebrating its twentieth anniversary in three weeks. How about a mix of red velvet and chocolate?"

"They'll be there, and so will I. Can't wait to see your mom again. She's a freaking hoot." Roxy gives a little wave as they take off.

Hoot. I shake my head as Marley plops down at the table.

"Sorry," I say stroking her long blonde hair. "Your sister had to bail."

Marley has the face of an angel and long, healthy curls as opposed to the chemically damaged carnage her sister wears like a bad wig. Marley is the anti-Jemma, and I mean that in the very best way.

"I'll have to call her and apologize." She looks to Annie. "I was down the street at Whitney Briggs signing up for my student orientation. I'm officially a college freshman." She rolls her eyes as if mocking herself in the process.

"Annie is starting in the fall, too," I say just as Annie whips out her phone and introduces herself to Marley through a series of spastic notes.

29

"I'll leave you two girls to get to know one another." I give Annie a quick hug before heading to the bar and taking a seat.

Baya and Bryson are still tongue tied in the darkest corner of the facility. Laney jets from table to table, beaming with a smile that Ryder himself put there. Even Annie and Marley seem to have a new connection that signals a great friendship on the horizon.

I spin in my seat and land my elbows over the dark, granite counter.

And here I am alone, once again.

Jemma's words come back to haunt me, Greasy D is in town.

I shake my head.

Sometimes alone is exactly what I want to be.

Holt

Izzy Sawyer.

Just breathe.

I try to keep my hard-on in check by focusing on the fact I still have another six hours left in my shift. Not that my shift ever really ends around here. I've been the director of operations for the last year and a half. Bryson is more or less eye candy for the female population, and I excuse it because, as my father bluntly put it, we don't want to burden him too much since he's in school. Not that he's still in school. He graduated last month along with some of our longtime friends. But he's been admitted to grad school, so he'll be making a U-turn come fall. No one is prouder of him than me, but it is a little strange to see people excelling in life while I'm stuck behind the counter, ironically right where I want to be.

Izzy sweeps her long, dark hair off her shoulders, and all I can think of is how bad I'd like to bury my face in it. Her lips give the perfect pout. Her eyes have always been a hypnotic glacial blue that not a person on the planet can keep from staring at. My dick perks to life again, and I take a deep breath. I haven't been within touching distance of Izzy Sawyer in months. And, God knows, my dick has been pointing in her direction for the last eight years. She and Jemma were two of the more infamous seniors of West Hollow Brook High. Of course, they were long gone by the time I hit high school. Too bad. I would have done any and everything to take Izzy Sawyer to prom. While Bryson and the rest of our buddies were drooling over the latest Hollywood hot mess, I was busy worshiping at the altar of Elizabeth Sawyer.

I take a breath and drum up the nerve to talk to her.

Laney rushes over and sits next to her sister, so I switch gears and pretend to rearrange the glasses set out under the bar.

"*So*, do you have a date for the engagement party?" Laney grabs her sister by the shoulder as if trying to shake an answer out of her.

"The party you just informed me about ten minutes ago?" Izzy belts out a laugh, and the sweet sound of her voice resonates right down to my boxers. "No, I'm afraid I don't move that fast."

"Jemma says you don't move at all these days." Laney rocks into her sister as if she's trying to get her to open up. I dated Laney once, but only because she was looking to drive Ryder off the deep end, and I'm pretty sure it worked. He still can't stand the sight of me. Ironic since he's good friends with my brother.

Izzy glances sideways at the exit. "Move—don't move—believe me I'm not crying over the lack of testosterone in my life, so both you and Jem can chill out. Yes, I'll be going to your engagement party *stag* and most likely your wedding, too. Is that grounds for disqualification? Too much reality for your fairytale lifestyle?"

"Very funny." Laney jumps to her feet. "Hey, I know"—her voice pitches with hope—"let me set you up on a few dates. Nothing serious, just some quick meet and greets. We can do it right here in the bar. You never know where things could lead."

"I know where things could lead—with me dead in a ditch." Izzy stabs the words at her sister before shooting me a look that suggests something akin to waterboarding is in her future. I give a quick nod and suddenly feel like an ass for standing here, listening.

"I guess. Whatever." Izzy gives in and shudders as if she just sunk a bad shot.

"Perfect!" Laney offers a quick kiss to her sister's cheek. "I'll catch you later. Tell Mom I said hi!" She takes off toward her tables once again.

"Yes, Holt, I still live with my mother." Izzy's lips curl with a sour smile, and even then she looks cute as hell.

"Nothing wrong with that." I make my way over and feel the air stifling. I've always felt as if a damn inferno was about to break out between us, and I can't for the life of me understand how this could be one-sided. Then again, I'm probably not in her league, so the entire inferno scenario is solely in my pants. Izzy is one of those untouchable girls reserved for the cream of the crop of which I'm the bottom of the barrel. "You might live with your mother, but I work at a bar. The end."

"What's this?" Her eyes brighten the exact shade of a sunny afternoon, and my cock is back to begging to be let out to play. Sorry, boy, this is one girl who will most likely never roll out the red carpet for you. "Are you trying to crash my pity party?"

"Consider it busted." I grab a glass and fill it with ice. "Any drink. It's on me."

"In that case, water."

"How about wine?" I'd uncork a bottle of the best vintage I have in stock for Izzy.

"No thanks, I don't really drink all that much. Sorry about the whiskey." She bites down on her cotton candy pink lip, and my gut starts to liquefy. Holy shit. Now I see why the universe never has us together more than once a year. I'd be a dead man if given a few more run-ins.

"No drinking, huh? I have the power to change that if you like." I'd rearrange the solar system for Izzy if she wanted.

"I'm good." She gives a sideways smile, and my head tilts in line with it. Damn. I've always wondered why my brother acted like a complete idiot around his girlfriend, Baya, and now I know—it can't be helped. When you find the one it's simply a knee-jerk reaction. Only I'm not Izzy's *one*, and that explains why she's looking at me like I'm some sort of bartending psychopath. "Anyway, I usually never touch the stuff, unless, of course, it's a special occasion, and, even then, I'm stuck on whiskey." She nods back to the table that holds her abandoned drink.

"Whiskey can be a tough place to start." It takes everything in me not to dive across the counter and shove my face in her neck just to see if she smells as good as I remember—sugar and spice and everything very fucking nice.

"Yeah, my dad—it was his signature drink. Most men prefer beer but not my father." She glances down at the counter and traces out a figure eight. "So what's new with you? Heard you just graduated. Your brother is getting hitched soon. Where's your significant other? She around?" Izzy pans the facility with those glowing eyes, and it makes my balls ache. All right, so my balls ache for her regardless, and it forces me to defer to my favorite lifelong mantra when I'm around her—just breathe— because, holy hell, Izzy Sawyer is beautiful. That's exactly what I used to remind myself each time I dropped Annie off and picked her up—breathe. If there's one woman who can take my breath away each and every time, it's Izzy. Always has been, always will.

Bryson nods to me from the far end of the bar as he picks up my slack.

"No significant other here." I try not to infer some underlying motive. The last thing I want to do is hit on Izzy as if she were just another barfly. "So I heard Laney." I try not to come across as an ass for listening in. "Sounds like you're about to hit the ground running."

"Ha!" She belts out a short-lived laugh. "As in running in the other direction. I doubt my Mr. Right is lurking in the mess she's about to sling my way."

35

I slide a glass of water to her, and she's quick to play with the straw. Her long, perfect fingers coil over the tip, each nail painted a bright cherry red. For a second I imagine plunging each one into my mouth, sucking her down before biting the tips ever so gently.

"Holt?" She catches my gaze.

"Yeah." Shit. Way to let her know you care.

"See? I can't even hold your attention. I'm about as exciting as watching paint dry. Anyway"—she hops down, and my heart breaks as she steps away from the bar—"I'm out of practice. I wouldn't even know what to say to someone."

"I can help with that." My heart rattles around in my chest unsure of what the hell I'm about to say next. "And, I promise, you're anything but boring. Any guy would be lucky to have you." Especially this one.

She shakes her head without thinking twice. "Trust me, I'm a charity case you want nothing to do with."

"Come by tomorrow night at seven, and I'll walk you through the basics. You'll be a pro by the time Laney sends you out into the cold, cruel world of dating. By the time I'm done, you'll have to fight them off with all four limbs. I'll teach you everything and anything you've ever wanted to learn." I steady my gaze over hers, and my heart aches because a part of me wishes she could see right through the charade I'm putting on. "You in?"

Her eyes widen, and she goes away for a moment.

"All right. I'm in." She sighs as she takes a step away. "I'll swing by at seven. Bring your pillow. You'll need it once I put you to sleep." She gives a little wink and heads off toward her sister. I watch as she sways those perfect hips, back and forth, back and forth.

A hand glides in front of my face, and I find Bryson standing there with a shit-eating grin.

"Sawyer still has you pussy whipped?"

"That about says it." I fling the dishtowel over my shoulder and watch as she embraces Laney before taking off. "Scored a date, too."

"More like a training session." That goofy grin slides off his face. "Heard the whole thing."

"Yeah, so what. I'd stand on my head and eat a bag of dog food if she wanted me to just as long as I could spend a few extra minutes with her."

"All hail Queen Izzy" He leans over the bar and looks from the empty doorway to me for a second. "Dude, are you going for the gold?" His demeanor shifts from playful to downright worried. "She's into thirty-year-olds and shit. You're a glorified teenager in her eyes."

"Doesn't bother me. So she's a few years older—five to be exact. And who the hell cares? Isn't Dad's newest squeezebox fifteen years his junior?" Or so he claims, we've yet to meet her. It makes me sick to think about it. Not the age difference—I'm still stuck on the fact he left my mother five years ago. I try to brush the memory from my mind. It was me who played a major role in their breakup, and I've hated myself for it ever since.

"I don't know." Bryson's gaze is still fixed at the far end of the bar. "I'd layoff if I were you."

"Would you have listened if I told you to layoff Baya? Hell, if I remember right, her brother told you just that, and it was the last thing you did."

"So you think she's your Baya, huh?" He huffs a quiet laugh. "I bet you a thousand bucks she's not your Baya. I seriously doubt she's going to give you the time of day let alone stick around long enough to stroke your ego or anything else, big bro." He swallows hard as if he's trying to let me down easy. I know for a fact he threw in that big bro comment to soften the blow. Every now and again he likes to flaunt the fact I've got fifteen minutes on him. "Look, I don't want to see you voluntarily putting your heart in a blender. I care about you. Let me set you up with someone. It'll be easy. They're already lining up around the block for you." He motions at the crowd of girls amassing at the far end of the bar. "Pick one. They're all dying to fall at your feet."

"I'll pass. And I'll pass on the bet. Don't you worry your pretty little head over where I put my heart." I'd let Izzy rip it out of my body and stomp on it with her pink ballet heel if she wanted. Hell, I'd encourage her to do it—hold it down for her.

I'd give Izzy anything—any part of me she wanted. Both Bryson and I know that.

My heart in a blender is just the first thing I'd offer.

And, if she'll let me, I'll throw in a whole lot more.

"You're really into her, aren't you?"

38

"God's honest truth right there." I stare out at the empty space left in her void and wonder if she could ever feel about me the way I do her.

"You should've offered to pick her up." He flexes a dry smile. "Sophomoric blunder."

"Didn't want to spook her." Izzy is as fragile as a dove. One overbearing move and I'm afraid she'll flutter away again, this time for good.

"Looks to me, she's got *you* pretty spooked." He flicks his towel at my chest before taking off. "Watch the ticker. If you're not careful, a girl like that can split it right in half."

I'd welcome it.

But then again, I'd welcome anything Izzy Sawyer has to offer.

2

Piece of Me

Izzy

Hey Dad,

Guess what?

Mom is up to her old tricks again, and by tricks I mean her quasi form of prostitution that involves non-paying customers. Living at the brothel is sort of wearing on me. You sure you don't want to pop in and alleviate some of this misery?

I know. You're never coming back. Sure wish you'd change your mind.

~Iz (Little Bit)

But then, you've forgotten who I am, haven't you?

୫୬୯୨

"Bashful, Sleepy, Sneezy, Grumpy," I call out as I rattle a bag of kibble, and right on cue all four jelly-bellied cat's waddle into the room with my mother on their heels.

"You really should upgrade your dining standards," I snark. My mother and I have been known to enjoy a healthy dose of banter. Her daily barbs assure me she's still breathing—and, in some small way, that she gives a damn.

"I wouldn't talk. You're just three cats away from a straight jacket." Mom walks by with her jet-black hair knifing out over the top of her head. A thick, blue headband is pressed into the center of her skull just trying to contain it. She's wearing her signature fuchsia lipstick and lavender bathrobe, both of which are nightly rituals. If my mother is anything she's immaculate at all hours of the day. She has a panache for matching her jewelry with her clothing, right down to her fingernail polish, shoes and purse. Unlike me who lives in stretch pants and a sports bra, but that's mostly because I'm at the studio 24/7.

"Straight jacket, huh? And here I thought I was three cats away from being a Disney Princess."

"Sorry, honey. To qualify I'd have to kick the bucket, and I don't plan on heading to the light just yet."

"Light? As in flame?" I tease. My mother is my life. I've ruined hers, and I plan on making up for it by keeping the promise I made to my father. My mother will never be alone. Laney doesn't come around much anymore, and I'm all she has left. Greasy D's ugly mug crops up in my mind, welcome as lighter fluid at a flash fire, and I push him right back out. "I saw Laney yesterday. She said to say hi."

"That's your sister's favorite song. Next time you see her, tell her to come by and tell me herself." She slaps the papers down on the table before taking a seat. "Damn bills." You'd think that was the proper name for the reckoning she partakes in each month to ensure the lights don't go out and we have an ample supply of hot water in the morning. "How did the classes go?" She asks as an afterthought.

Mom's been away from the dance studio for weeks now ever since she turned her ankle. The doctor's been after her to lose some weight, but, by the looks of how she's eyeing that box of Yo-Ho's next to her, it's a farfetched idea.

She reaches for the carton as if reading my mind.

"The doctor said—"

She holds a Yo-Ho up victoriously. "The doctor can pry this out of my cold, dead hands."

"He might get the chance."

My mother never listens. I learned that the hard way the summer I turned eighteen. I brush the memory out of my mind before it ever gets the chance to fully form.

"Classes were fine. Bella wants a raise. She says—"

"Tell her to get in line." She lifts the stack of envelopes once again and snarls. "I can't stand this bullshit anymore. Some days I think it's just not worth the headache." She pulls the hair at her temples. "It's either

43

this mother isn't happy with the coaching—or that one wants her daughter to have a solo every damn week—and I've got fifteen building inspectors breathing down my neck nagging at me to make repairs, or they're going to nail the doors shut. It's all a load of bullcrap if you ask me." She bites the Yo-Ho's chocolate head off as if she means business. "Donny and I were talking about firing up the motorhome. What do you think of that?"

My heart stops. "Donny" is a moron who, if memory serves correct, believes in tweaking my ass when he's wasted out of his mind on a bender.

"What is it exactly that draws you to him?" For a woman who seems to have every single answer in life, she can never really figure out men. Over the years, Mom's rendition of a good catch has been—same loser, different body. If there's a bad batch of assholes out there, rest assured, my mother has plowed through them all.

"He's tall, dark, and dangerous, and he gives me the time of day."

"So you're settling." At least she got the dangerous part right.

"You wish. Bobbie Sawyer never settles." She darts a pudgy finger at me. "That man is a saint for putting up with her, what with all the foul language and condescending remarks—and those are just the verbal love pats she directs at him. Any lesser of a man would have long since sliced his own balls off before hightailing out of town. He gets her. He knows her love language is lethal and that she's not afraid to abuse it."

"Nice. And, by the way, speaking about yourself in third person is creepy, knock it off, or I'll flex my power to have you committed." I'm only half-kidding. Greasy D is an asshole. The D might as well stand for douche—although, I'll give him points for dealing with my mother. And if he ever shows up smashed and tries to cop a feel, I'll be the one slicing his balls off. I'm not some helpless teenager cowering in the corner anymore, hoping he won't hit on my sister or me. In fact, if things get crazy, I might slice off his dick for kicks, too.

I fill the cats bowls and give them each a quick scratch behind the ears. Three orange Tabbies and a white Persian. They're my babies, my family, and no matter how insane I look by collecting them en masse, I'm their furless mommy for the long haul. Besides, if it weren't for their fluffy warm coats, who would heat the sheets with me at night? It's a sad day when you're able to admit the only attention you get in bed is of the feline variety. Speaking of attention...

"So"—I stand and arch my back until my lungs fill with the unfortunate scent of tuna and salmon—"I'm headed to the Black Bear again. Laney is determined to set me up on a series of bad memories in the making. I thought I'd go ahead and humor her once or twice."

"Bad memories as in bad dates? *Blind* dates?" Her sea blue eyes dart up to mine. "So that's what it's come to, huh?" She plucks another Yo-Ho out of the box and pulls back the wrapper like peeling a banana. "Well, good riddance. Maybe we'll both get some action for once. I'm tired of watching those damn cats rut around the house like this is some sort of feline brothel. Where's *our* rutting? Where's *our* cat on a hot tin roof moment?"

"I'm leaving now. And you can add another word to the make Izzy-evacuate-from-the-room list." I almost trip over the small herd of felines twirling around my feet. If anything my mother doesn't mince words.

"What word is that? Rutting or brothel?" Her voice fades as I pick up my purse and throw on my jacket. She stagers out to the living room. "Where you headed?"

"I told you, the Black Bear. Holt Edwards is giving me a few pointers on how to improve my game."

"Annie's brother? That little shit?" She digs her palm into her eye as if the idea gave her a migraine.

"That's the one."

"I'll bet he's got a pointer for you—in his *boxers*. I told you, years ago, we should have gotten a restraining order against that twerp."

I laugh opening the door, and my heart stops cold. My mother had the restraining order part right, just not against Holt.

"Well, look what we've got here." Greasy D growls while riding his gaze up and down my body—pausing at all the inappropriate points of interest. "If it isn't the bell of the ball." Greasy touches his hand to my cheek, and I'm quick to bat it away.

I bolt past him.

"See you later, Mom." But with him here, home is the last place I want to be.

Ever.

Holt Edwards might just get more of me than he bargained for.

ᏚᏓᏨ

The Black Bear is jam-packed with scantily dressed bodies. A giant, life-size bear stands at the entrance, holding a hand painted sign that reads *Open mike night! All coed crooners welcome.* And, by the looks of things, they showed up in droves.

"Perfect," I mutter under my breath. I started nursing a headache the second I left the house—can't wait to round out the night listening to some college sophomore squeak out the latest not-so-greatest hits. Can't wait for my brain to explode and put me out of my misery. My mother flashes through my mind. God, I hope that man is decent to her this time. I close my eyes a moment because I already know where this crazy train is headed.

"Hey, beautiful." A warm arm finds its way around my waist, and I look up to find a freshly pressed and dressed—drop my panties to the floor in salute of his eminence—Holt Edwards. My heart thumps in my chest. The subtle scent from his cologne is enough to make me swoon, but Holt has the face of an angel, or with that slightly peppered scruff he's sporting—a devil.

"Why are you always so nice to me?" I meant to say hello, but the question bubbled out instead.

His eyes widen as if it was the last thing he expected. "Because you deserve it."

Holt bears into me with a soul-melting look that makes my insides cinch until I can't catch my next breath. His cut features—those glowing eyes—it's becoming obvious this was a big mistake.

"I'm the last person you should be wasting your time with." I swallow hard. "You sure you don't have better things to do?" Already three different girls have walked by outright gawking at him. "Honestly, you don't have to baby sit me tonight."

"Baby sit?" Holt steps in close, his eyes sear over mine, and, for the first time, in a long while I can feel the heat spreading through my body like a molten tidal wave, slow and determined to hit all the right spots. His sweet cologne infiltrates my senses—sandalwood and cinnamon. He takes in a breath, and his chest stops just shy of touching mine. Holt Edwards is all man. Forget those preconceived notions I've had about him over the years. He's grown into his own, and, God help me, because I very much approve. He leans in further, and, for a fleeting moment, I think he's going to kiss me. "I promise you, Iz"—he whispers right over my lips, and I'm tempted to steal it from him anyway—"there's not a single place I'd rather be."

He reaches over and opens the door. Holt picks up my hand and leads us out into the quiet night away from the crooning coeds and their obnoxious vocal cords.

"No Black Bear tonight?" I bite down on my lip as he leads me over to his truck. My hand burns from his touch. A wave of heat travels up to my chest, and I savor it. I can't get over the fact he just picked up my hand like it was no big deal. But then to Holt it probably isn't. I'm guessing he's a bit more liberal than I am when it comes to dolling out physical affection. I take in the sensation of his thick fingers closing over mine, the warmth of his flesh, and savor the contact high. I can't remember the last time I held a boy's hand—most likely because it's never really happened. That night flashes through my mind like a jag of lightning, and I blink it away. I'm not inviting any of those memories to the party. Tonight is about forgetting—about learning new things with Holt, like holding hands and dating.

"No Black Bear." He opens the door to his truck and helps me up before jumping in on the other side. "You mind if I take you somewhere quiet?"

"Please take me somewhere quiet. You're welcome to keep me there if you like." I press my head into the seat and relax for the first time in what feels like years. "My mother's ex has reared his ugly head, and I want no part of that action."

"Got it." He winces at the road. I take him in like this. Holt is confident behind the wheel. His strong arms sit low as he navigates us through the twisted roads of Hollow Brook. He has an overall comforting presence about him. "I was thinking a nice restaurant. Maybe hit downtown Jepson?"

"For me? Don't bother." I'd feel terrible if he insisted on paying. "I'm sort of a drive-through kind of girl anyway."

"You're worth it, Iz." He glances over with his brows knit a moment. "And I'm here because I want to be."

"You're here because I'm a basket case you've decided to take under your wing. I'm the reason you're probably not going to get laid tonight." My stomach bisects with heat. Crap. Did I just go there? "What am I saying? You probably have a line of girls snaking around your apartment just waiting for the call. My bad—sorry."

He gives a slight chuckle. "As far as I know, there's no line." He nods up at the rows of fast food restaurants coming upon us. "Which one looks good?"

"I don't know. It's always the same stuff. I wish they had one that specialized in a good grilled cheese sandwich. Sometimes that's all a girl really needs. God knows I'd do anything for one right about now."

"It's your lucky night because I know just the place." The truck kicks into gear, and we bypass the rows of heart-clogging cholesterol and empty calories, trading them for a far less nutritious fare—which happens to be my all time favorite.

"Who serves grilled cheese sandwiches in Hollow Brook?"

His lips curl on the sides. His lids slit low and seductive as he cuts me a look. "I do."

ജാരു

We drive up to a large boxy apartment lined with acacia trees and the occasional trashcan set out front. The building sits wide, almond-colored with a dark brown trim and looks more homey than it does industrial unlike so many of the newer construction high-rises that seem to be taking over this college town.

"So this is home?"

"The one and only."

Holt insists I walk up the stairs first and unlocks the door off the stairwell. "After you."

"You're a real gentlemen. You're spoiling me, by the way. Laney's army of blind mice are going to have to work twice as hard to impress me." I glance around at the neat surroundings, the minimalist furnishings. "Wow, fireplace, stainless appliances. You're really living in style." I give his ear a little tug without putting much thought into it, and an errant spark flies between us unexpected as a deer on the highway. "So when can I move in?"

"I'm ready when you are, sweetheart." He growls it out low, and—oh my God, what have I gotten myself into?

"Yeah, well"—I clear my throat—"you'll get tired of all my girly things taking up real estate in your bathroom. I hand wash all my personals." His face blooms with a dark smile. Obviously, I'm not helping. "Trust me, you'd kick me out first chance you get." I stray deeper into his apartment, across the dark wood floor that leads to the plush-piled carpet in the living room—the kind that invites you to kick your shoes off and dig your toes in for a while.

"I don't think I'd get tired of your girly things." He gives a grin that comes as quick as it goes. "In fact, I think a few 'personals' would brighten things up around here." He holds my gaze steady like a dare, and a series of goose bumps trail up my arms.

Holt makes his way to the kitchen, and I follow. His tall frame commands attention in this tiny space as he maneuvers around until he has a frying pan heating on the stove and a stack of sliced bread ready to go.

"Let me help." I offer, taking the cheese out of the package—smoked Gouda, my all time favorite.

"Let's do this."

Holt and I work side by side until we've amassed enough grilled cheese sandwiches to outfit a small platoon. Every now and again our shoulders bump, and I feel his strong as steel body against mine. My flesh burns from head to toe. I've done a lot of deflecting in my day, but I don't ever remember wanting to lean in and touch someone—to spread my hands wide over their chest—the way I do now. But, then, this is Holt Edwards of the notorious, womanizing Edwards'. It's no surprise he has the art of seduction down to a science. I bet grilled cheese sandwiches factor into the break down of how fast he can land a girl horizontal. Too bad for him it won't work on this girl, or, rather, too bad for me.

Holt pulls out a couple of sodas, and we head to the fireplace where he starts a roaring blaze quicker than I can protest the romantic idea. We take a seat on the carpet across from one another.

"So"—he lands the grilled works of art smack between us, rising high like a stack of dairy-filled pancakes—"tell me why a hot girl like you would ever need tips on dating." He gives the idea of a smile, and my heart takes off like a greyhound at the track.

"First, I'm not hot," I correct. "I own a mirror. And I happened to see enough of the coed offerings tonight at the Black Bear to know there are far more combustible prospects out there. I can never compete with that. Second, I just don't date." I take a bite out of the masterpiece Holt and I whipped up and give an audible moan of approval. My head arches back as I let the ooey gooey goodness melt down my throat a moment.

His mouth opens as if he's about to say something, but I've rendered him speechless, or at least I'd like to believe I have that kind of power.

"Izzy." He leans in with that serious demeanor that my insides have quickly become addicted to. The entire lower half of my body just detonated like a flare gun. It scares me on a primal level to know that Holt has that kind of effect on me. "You're legendary in Hollow Brook. No offense, but you've sponsored a boner in every guy that ever went to West. You're the *it* girl. The fantasy of every boy you've ever met, and, for the life of me, I can't figure out how you're not fighting off men."

"Oh, I've definitely engaged in mortal combat a time or two." My eighteenth birthday comes to me like the lash of a whip, and I close my eyes a moment.

"You okay?" He places his hand gently over my arm and leans in just enough. I can tell Holt really does care.

"I'm fine. Let's talk about you. So what did you major in?"

"Life." He takes a huge bite of his sandwich then polishes off half his soda. "I didn't go the college route."

"Oh, but I thought— I just assumed because Bryson went..."

"I know. It's okay. It's something I couldn't wrap my head around at the time. I had some things I needed to sort out. Anyway, I think I'm okay without it."

"It's not for everybody," I offer a little too quick. "I mean, I didn't go."

"You didn't go?" His forehead wrinkles as if this somehow takes the sheen off who he thinks I am, and it should. I'm a far cry from this teen idol he's painted me out to be.

"I didn't. And I certainly don't judge anyone who chooses not to. I promise, there's life outside those ivy-covered walls. I'm living proof." Sort of.

He gives a slow nod. His eyes ride up and down my body with that elevator stare, and, I can't help think any moment now he's going to realize what a mistake this is and show me the door.

"So, tell me"—he starts—"why aren't you out there breaking hearts like you're supposed to?"

I finish off my sandwich and wash it down with my Cherry Coke, trying to find just the right lie to feed him.

"I'm...really busy. I've all but taken over the studio." The truth lingers just beyond my touch like a fur-lined beast waiting to devour me. But that's as close as I can get. Besides, Holt fed me the best damn grilled cheese sandwich I could ever hope to put in my stomach. There's no way I could ever lie to him.

"Busy, huh?" He tips his head back, eyeing me through heavily slotted lids. "So you're up for some pointers?"

"From you?" I sketch his mouth out into my memory. Holt has lush, full lips that you would never think a man would have, and I savor their effigy for later. "I'll take them all night long." Crap. Did I just say that? My eyes widen then retract. I try to play it off as if it's no big thing—but, God, I'm going to give him the wrong idea. He's going to think I'm some kind of a predator who tricked him into taking me to his sexual lair and demanded grilled cheese sandwiches in exchange for lewd acts. At least that's what Jemma would do.

He bears into me with his eyes slit with desire. That intense gaze of his burns through me like acid, and my cheeks catch fire from the inside. Holt is a master at what he does, and, any moment now, I'm going to voluntarily get in that line of girls just waiting to jump into his bed. My breathing becomes erratic. I lean in on impulse then straighten. What am I thinking? This is Holt. This is *me*. Me, the virgin. I don't jump in beds. I'm not just some girl he's picked up at a party. I'm a certifiable mess, and if he knew how truly deformed I was on the inside, he wouldn't be eyeing me as if he'd like a bite.

"When was the last time you kissed anybody?" He asks point blank. My entire body flushes with heat. My toes curl without meaning to, and I can't catch my breath. "I think we should start there."

"Holt?" I swallow hard, trying to ignore the boulder lodging in my throat. "Would you mind giving me a ride back to my car?"

Holt

Sunday night, Mom invites us all to dinner. Baya and Bryson are hanging out on the couch watching some old flick. Annie is in the kitchen with Mom. Here I am alone, wondering what the fuck happened last night and how the hell to fix it.

Nitro, my mother's black lab, hops up and nestles next to me. Why do I get the feeling there's something allegorical happening here.

"So, what gives?" Bryson knocks my leg off the coffee table with his foot. "I asked you a half hour ago how it went with Iz."

I take a hard sniff trying to come up with something that won't make me feel like an ass. "Just hung out. Took her to my place and had a quick bite."

"A quick bite?" Baya looks to Bryson before breaking out in giggles. "That's a new way to put it."

"It wasn't that kind of bite. It was completely platonic." The last thing I need is Izzy thinking I'm spreading rumors. It's obvious she's got some issues when it comes to men. Either that or I make one hell of a lousy grilled cheese sandwich. "You know anything about her?" I nod over to Baya. I know for a fact Baya is tight with Laney. She might be able to add a little clarity to the mystery.

"Just met her. Well, I met her once before when Roxy puked on her shoes, but that lasted about five seconds."

Much like our non-date.

"I know Laney's been actively looking for someone to set her up with," she continues. "In fact, she mentioned she had next Friday night all mapped out for her."

"Nice." And there you go.

Bryson pulls Baya in tight, and a wave of jealousy prickles through me. A part of me wishes it were me and Izzy sitting on that couch. Funny thing is she's the only girl I've ever wanted that with.

"You know"—my brother holds up a finger—"Ryder mentioned something once about her having a cat collection. He said if ever there was a crazy cat lady in the making it was Izzy."

"No shit. Cats?" Not that it's any crime, but it's painting a picture. I shake my head stumped as hell. Izzy is a goddess that deserves to be worshipped nightly. I wonder what's really eating at her. I don't buy for a second that she's more interested in cats than men. Then it hits me like a ton of shit bricks. What if she's into chicks? A cloud of grief lays over me. That's one bill I can't fill. Crap. I don't even want to go there.

"Dinner," Mom sings from the dining room, and we head over. There's a man by her side and a woman by his, and it takes a second to register exactly who he is because I haven't seen his face in this house since I was in high school.

"Dad?" Annie says without hesitating. It's so rare she vocalizes anymore. A few kids made fun of her a couple times, and she's been nothing but whispers and sign language ever since.

We head over and crowd our father with a good old-fashioned group hug. It takes a second for it to sink in that he's brought a plus one. A thin, exceptionally young brunette stands sheepishly off to the side, and I'm assuming she's Dad's new main squeeze even though we haven't formally been introduced.

"Look who's back." I motion with my hand a little more aggressively than necessary. At the house we sign as much as possible. It's natural as breathing, not to mention we'd never want Annie to feel left out. "What's going on?" I give his arm a light swat as we make our way to our seats.

"Does something need to happen for me to have a nice Sunday dinner with my family?" He offers that signature politician grin he's famous for—lying through his teeth while mugging for the camera, or, in this case, our attention.

"Traditionally." Mom averts her eyes before offering her own signature grin, the one she throws out like a barb when she's good and pissed—like now.

"Let's hold off on the sarcasm, Miranda. You mind?" He gives her a slimy wink. "Just one night." He glances around the table. "Everyone, I'd like for you to meet Jenny. Jenny and I have been seeing one another for a while, and I thought it would be good for us all to sit down and get acquainted." He nods over at Baya. "And I see there are some people I've yet to meet, myself."

Bryson segues into the intros, and we start in on dinner. Twice I catch Jenny checking out my brother and me. I know that look. She likes what she sees. Swear to God, I've got a couple years on her. Mom said she was a little older than me, but it's obvious Jenny, here, is barely street legal. What the hell does she want with someone like my dad anyway? It's obvious she thinks the bars are some giant cash cow that will pave her closet with designer handbags and shoes. I've got news for her. The bars aren't oozing money. Actually, that's spot on. They're hemorrhaging like there's no tomorrow. It's a fucking sieve, and if we don't take care of things soon, we'll all be out on the streets looking for a sugar daddy.

Mom touches her hand to mine while Bryson and Baya carry on a full-blown conversation with Dad.

"You okay?" She mouths.

"I'm fine."

I can see the hurt in her eyes. The betrayal is still as fresh as the day he left. My appetite cuts out, and I think I'm next. I push my plate back, and Dad is quick to eye it.

"Before we lose anyone," he clears his throat— "Jenny and I have an announcement."

Crap. I shoot a look to Mom, and her jaw clenches. Her hands knot up in fists. I've done this to her. You can place the blame of what comes next right on my fucked-up shoulders.

"We're going to make it official." Jenny squeals like one of Nitro's chew toys before holding up the rock on her hand.

"And there it is," Bryson whispers just under his breath.

Nice to know we think alike, too.

The rest of the night goes off like a bomb, and even Annie looks as if she's ready to slaughter our father with a butter knife.

Yup, all my fault.

ജി

After the fuck fest that was dinner, I take off and head for the hills, otherwise known as anywhere but here. That night from long ago comes to the surface, and I try to push it away, submerge it right back down where it belongs, in the filth and the mire, the forever castoff of my mind. I've done some stupid shit in my day, but that night—that damn night changed the way I breathe. It took what my parents once had and flushed it down the toilet—flushed my future right along with it.

Izzy pops back into my mind and a flood of relief fills me. It's funny because all these years I've held onto her like some sort of life raft, and now she's really in it—sort of. Not that she'll most likely ever speak to me again after what happened at my apartment, but, thanks to Baya, I know just where to find her next Friday night—at the

Black Bear on her first blind date. I'd love to take her out myself sometime—maybe take her for a ride on the boat.

I drive through downtown Jepson on my way home. I know for a fact Laney and Ryder live here somewhere in one of these high-rises. Wish I knew which one. I'd swing by and see if I can get anything out of them about Izzy without being too obvious.

A dull laugh rattles through me as I make my way home. I'm not sure I can hide my feelings for Iz much longer.

Sooner than later it'll be apparent to everyone how I feel about Izzy Sawyer. But I don't think anyone gives a rat's ass one way or the other.

I just hope Izzy does.

At the end of the day, she's the only one that matters.

That's been true since the first day I laid eyes on her.

3

Desperate and Dating

Izzy

Hey Dad,

How's it going?

Me? I'm still royally goofing up my life. It's called paralysis by analysis. Sometimes I want to move in a different direction, but then I start to overthink things and my brain gets fried. Has that ever happened to you? I guess I'll never know. I have so many questions for you with nothing but blank space on the other side of them. You would think I'd be used to the nothingness of it all by now, but my heart has foolishly saved a place for you, and all I have to fill it is grief. For the record, I don't believe in "good" grief. It's all bad—right down the very last drop. I should know, I'm still grieving for you.

~Izzy

There have been plenty of times I've wanted to wring Laney's neck over the years—mostly for borrowing my clothes without asking, but I have a feeling by the time this night is through, I'll have amassed an entire new list of reasons.

The Black Bear Saloon is a metropolis of every STD known to man and some that have yet to be discovered. Laney seats me in a dark booth toward the back of the booze-riddled establishment as I await my potential Mr. Friday Night Right.

I keep an eye on everyone who enters the facility, but mostly it's groups of girls—guys with their arms already wrapped around a coed for the night. Not a single person walks in alone—another sign that I'm a basket case because that just so happens to be the way I walked in.

Holt catches my eye from the bar, and my heart stops. My face floods with heat as I quickly look away. Crap. I'm still not over the trauma of ditching him for no apparent reason last week. Well, other than the fact I wanted that kiss. I wanted to press my lips to his and feel the softness for myself—to set my tongue loose in his mouth and have the thrill of him doing the same. I wonder where it would have gone from there—how far things could have escalated if I blew the ceiling off my self-inflicted boundaries. A vision of us rolling around naked on that shag carpet of his runs through my mind, and I don't fight it. I let that slow burn in my gut increase in ferocity until I'm sure my body is about to combust into flames. Holt is a wildfire waiting to happen. He's also a saint for volunteering to teach me the basics, but a part of me wants more, and I can't figure out what to do with that.

I glance back, and Holt gives a brief smile. His muscles ripple out from under his Black Bear T-shirt like the thick roots of a hundred-year-old tree. I lift my fingers in a mock wave while openly studying his biceps as if I had just discovered new terrain that I'd like to map out with my lips. Holt hasn't taken those pale gray eyes off me yet. He looks hungry—malnourished as far as his sexual appetite goes, and it's as if he's fixed his sights on a scrumptious meal in the shape of my body.

Every inch of me quivers at the prospect. Could I do that? Am I even remotely ready? Just what is it that I'm waiting for?

Holt's grin expands as he makes his way over. The music shifts to a far more moody song, and suddenly I'm hopped up on adrenaline and false bravado thinking he might ask me to dance. Hell, I think I'll ask *him* to dance. Just something platonic to wet my appetite for the things that he might be willing to give me.

"Izzy!" Laney sings in that overly cheery way that lets me know she wants something, and judging by the tall Slim Jim of a man standing by her side, the thing she wants most is for me to join myself at the hip with someone of the opposite gender. "This is *Marty McMullen*." She says his name as if there was some underlying meaning in it. She presses a hand into his T-shirt, and it concaves where his chest should be. His hair is long and shaggy. He's skin over bone for the most part but defined in that sinewy way that cyclists usually are. "He's a sports enthusiast! Just like you!" She deposits him into the seat across from me. "Well, I'll let you two kids get to know each other. Drinks are on me."

He holds up a long, thin finger. "Just a beer is fine."

"I'll have one, too." Wait, I'm driving. And I don't drink. "Make it a virgin."

Laney sucks in her cheeks. "One non-alcoholic beer and one regular."

"You know." I glance back at the bar where Holt is in action as a crowd of blondes bombard him with their over-glossed lips and Victoria's Secret enhanced décolleté. "Never mind." I almost said whiskey. Almost.

Laney takes off, and for three solid seconds I will myself to teleport anywhere but here. What the hell was I thinking? I don't do blind dates. Hell, I don't *date*.

"I hiked up Daringer Peak last weekend." He starts in with his mile-high achievement. "You a hiker?"

And so it begins, a forty-minute montage of all his daredevil feats that have taken place over every corner of God's green globe. I've long since knocked back my near-beer, and he's yet to touch his, but swear to God if he drones on, I might have to start damaging my liver just to keep up.

"This is really great." He comes out of his vested monologue after running down the bullet points of his titanic list of achievements. "We need to get together again. I think we're really hitting it off." His Adam's apple travels up and down the length of his neck like a broken elevator. "You up for a night hike? I know a cliff side just past the Witch's Cauldron that's vertical as shit." His eyes bug out at the prospect, and, for a fleeting moment, I wonder if I should be alarmed. "We can hit it right now!" He leans in, hitching his thumb toward the exit. Holy crap. They say never let an abductor take you to a second location. I'm pretty sure that's one rule I should abide by tonight. "I've got my climbing gear in the trunk." He's halfway out of his seat while I screw myself into mine.

"In the trunk?" I'm betting he has a Hefty bag and shovel back there, too. Where the heck did Laney find this one? And what exactly are her requirements for this little charade? All limbs accounted for? A basic eye exam? I'm thinking a Rorschach inkblot test could have taken us far.

"If you're not down for that, we could do a run. I've got a pair of night vision goggles in the trunk, too!" His breathing picks up pace. "We could hit the beach." His eyes bulge as if it were the greatest idea in the world—never mind the fact it's just this side of freezing. That's nature's way of giving June the finger. "There's nothing like getting the sand between your toes—just taking off down the shore like a fucking bullet!" His hand jets past my face, and, swear to God, he was inches from smacking me in the eye.

Crap.

I do a quick sweep of the bar for my psychotic baby sis, but she's nowhere to be found—blissfully oblivious to my newfound terror of all the things that might be lurking in *Marty McMullen's* trunk. My eyes snag on a familiar brassy blonde—Jemma.

"Or hell"—he digs his fingers into his temples—"I don't know why I didn't think of this before. We got all those damn dormitories right down the street!" He sweeps my elbow off the table. "Fire escapes!"

"Fire escapes?" Dear God. I need a fire escape.

"There's no greater rush than climbing those fuckers at midnight." The veins on the side of his neck bulge like garden snakes trying to escape their imprisonment.

"I don't think so. I'm not wearing the right shoes." I sling my purse strap over my shoulder and prepare for my own escape. I'm going to string Laney up on a fire escape by midnight if this doesn't end soon.

"All right, look." He scoots in close and snatches me up by the arm. His fingers close over me tight as a coil.

"Don't touch me," I breathe the words out, almost inaudible. That fated night comes back to me in jags. *Don't touch me! My mom will be home any minute. I said stop!*

"We should go for a drive down to Jenson's Lake. I've got a kayak hidden in the brush—" He buries his face in my neck, and I gag on my next breath. "The things I'd like to do to you."

A pair of strong arms pluck him off and send him flying.

"Get the fuck *out!*" Holt roars before pulling me from my seat and cradling my face in his hands. "You all right?" His steely eyes settle on mine, and something deep inside my soul melts. I want to bury myself in his chest and cry rivers because I'm anything but all right.

"Yes. I promise, I'm fine." The lie corks from my throat like a raft. "He was just getting worked up."

"He's a notorious cokehead. I think Laney needs a little help vetting the crew." He glances over his shoulder, and we watch as coked-up Marty blasts his way to the exit.

"Nice." Figures. Laney is scraping the bottom of the barrel, most likely because the rest of the barrel is taken.

Holt gives the idea of a smile, his eyes never leaving mine. "You look beautiful."

The heat rushes to my cheeks. "You always say that."

"I always mean it." He's still cradling my face in his hands like he's going to kiss me, and a primal part of me is screaming for him to do it.

The music dies down, and a stagnant silence crops up between us. Holt's chest expands wide as the world as he leans in.

"You smell nice." He pulls his hands away, and my insides cinch because every last part of my body was hoping for something more.

"Thank you." The music starts up again—loud and atrocious, as the crowd goes wild on the dance floor. "I'm sorry about last weekend."

Laney and Jemma burst into our little corner of the world, each with equally wild-eyed expressions.

"What the hell happened?" Laney points hard at the door. "I just saw Marty leave nursing his balls. Tell me you didn't knee him."

"She didn't," Holt answers. "I did."

"Nice touch." I place my hand over his back, and an electric current travels up my arm, setting off a series of sparks throughout my shoulder. I can feel the tension snapping as my veins snake out of control like downed power lines. Holt is rewiring me from the inside. He's putting all the connections right back where they belonged, where they once were before my eighteenth birthday, and I marvel at the power he has over me.

"Well, well." Jemma steps in, eyeing the metric distance between our bodies or lack thereof. "What have we got here?" Her lips expand right off her face with that shit-eating grin. Swear to God if she says the word cougar, I'll make sure another body hangs from that fire escape I'm about to swing Laney on.

"Just a friend helping a friend." Holt is quick to answer. He flings his bar towel over his shoulder and bears into me with those sea silver eyes. "Let me know if there's anything you need." There's a sadness in his tone, something morose as if on some level he knows I would never take him up on his offer. He takes off toward the bar, and my gaze drifts to his Levis.

Laney waves her hand over my face. "Earth to Izzy. Okay, so Marty was sort of a creep, but it's good that we got that out of the way. While you were over here sorting the sheep from the goats, I found another hot prospect."

"The sheep from the goats?" I interrupt before she can hit the gas once again on this crazy train. "I, my dear sister, was busy conducting an amateur psychiatric evaluation and judiciously weighing the prospect of my short-term safety."

"It's all in the past." She's quick to brush off my quest for sanity. "Next Wednesday night, you've got a molten hot date with Dr. Cliff Lancaster."

"A doctor?" I scoff. "Anyone can be a doctor in a bar, Laney."

Jemma pushes me out of the way. "Are we talking G.P. or some of that metaphysical bullshit?"

"Neither." Laney gives a sliver of a smile. "He's a podiatrist. And I did some fact checking. Two guys from the track team testified to this. I swear, this one is golden, and have I mentioned he has the eyes of a god? I'm telling you, Iz, this is the one."

"Right." I cut a quick glance to the bar where Holt is busy tending to an entire harem of wannabe bedmates. There's only one man with the eyes of a god around here, and I happen to be looking at him.

"Oh, hon"—Jemma shakes her head at Laney—"you don't know your sister at all, do you? Sometimes it takes more than the *one* to set a girl's heart straight."

"I know my sister plenty." She bats off Jemma's remark. "Tomorrow night is the big party. Be here at six. We're serving dinner. You're welcome too, Jem." Laney gives a little wave from over her shoulder as she swims back into the crowd.

"*Rwarrr.*" Jemma purrs in my ear as we both stare at the hottest bartender around. "Looks to me like you've already found the *one*." She mocks Laney in the process.

Jemma doesn't believe in the *one*, other than the one right now. "Go on and get him, hon. God knows you're starving for that kind of attention. Nothing a little cougar action can't cure. I bet he can prescribe just the right shots to get you rollin' around his bed like a kitten." She tweaks my ribs, and I jump. "You know you want to."

"Would you stop?" I bat her away like a gnat. "I'm not there yet."

"Is this about—"

"Yes." I cut her off before she speaks it into existence. Years ago, when I told her what happened, she promised she'd never repeat it, not even to me. "It's always about that." I shake my head. "I gotta go. I've got about four of my own starved kittens just waiting to roll around in bed with me."

That's about all the action I'll ever get because I can't breathe anytime a man comes near me. I'm broken—an old machine with faulty wiring.

I head out without bothering to say goodbye to Holt.

He doesn't need someone like me in his life.

I'm pretty sure no one does.

Holt

Marty Flying High McMullen. Who the hell would set Izzy up with that fool? Laney, that's who. I spot Izzy darting out the exit and tell Cole to man the fort.

I thread my way through the crowd and land outside where the night jasmine lights up the air with its sweet perfume. Not as sweet as Izzy. It took all my self-control not to bury my face in her hair. She holds the scent of lilacs in springtime. That was a contact high right there.

"Izzy," I shout as she's about to take off in her faded blue Honda Civic. She starts up the engine and rolls down the passenger window.

"Did I leave something behind? A douchebag trying to stick his tongue in my ear?" You can see the sarcasm dripping from her lips, and, ironically, I want to lick that up, too. Hell, I'd lick up anything Izzy offered.

"Just me." I give a sheepish grin. Her dark hair flows over her shoulder like a smoky, black river. Her eyes cut through the dark like twin stars born at midnight. How the hell is she ever single? "You up for a couple quick pointers?"

"Do they involve Tae Kwon-Do?"

"Close. Sushi."

Her lips crimp as she considers this. "Done. But we take separate cars."

"Getaway vehicle." I mock shoot her. "I like a girl with a plan."

I hop in my truck, and she follows me to downtown Jepson to one of the hottest new restaurants in town. It costs a mint to eat here, but it's quiet, and dark, and the electric blue haze that glows from the up lights matches her eyes. I wouldn't want to take her anywhere else.

I park and follow the scarf of her perfume as we head inside, opting to sit at the bar.

"So what gives?" She raises a brow, and my dick perks to attention. There's never been a whole lot Izzy had to do to get my attention or that of any member of my anatomy.

"Meaning?"

"Why are you my knight in shining armor lately?"

"Maybe I've always been, and it's just taken you this long to notice." Great. Make her sound like she's not observant enough. I wouldn't blame her for bolting right now.

Her mouth opens as if she's about to say something, and she's quick to close it. "I don't need a knight, Holt." She drops her gaze for a second. "But thank you."

The waitress comes by and asks if we're ready to order.

"I think I need a sec." Izzy raises a long, slender finger, and I can't help but imagine slipping it past my lips. Every last part of her makes my mouth water, and her pretty pink fingernails are no exception.

I go ahead and put in my order as Izzy bites down over her finger, still studying the menu.

"Hawaiian roll." She shakes her head. "Rainbow." She gives a nervous laugh. "Definitely a rainbow roll."

"Great!" The waitress snaps my menu and reaches for Izzy's, but she's quick to pull it back.

"On second thought, make it an eel roll—extra sauce."

"You got it." The waitress tries to pry the menu from Izzy's hand, and a tugging war ensues.

"Maybe I should stick with the Hawaiian?"

"How about all three?" I suggest. "I'll help polish them off." I was just being polite by not ordering half the menu anyway.

Izzy gives a slight nod.

"Sorry," she whispers as the waitress disappears. "That's me in a nutshell. I can't seem to take a step forward without taking two steps back."

"Baby steps. Sometimes that's the quickest way to move anywhere."

"Baby steps." She lowers her lashes and swallows hard. "You always know the right thing to say." Izzy looks up at me with a question in her eyes, but she won't give it.

I rock my shoulder into hers. "All right, fill in the gaps for me. You graduated high school—that's about as far we got the other night. You're still at the studio and what else? Any bad breakups you want to tell me about?" Shit. I'm pretty sure digging up bad memories is no way to break the ice. Leave it to me to put the night in the crapper long before our food ever arrives.

"Nope. I bet you can trump me in that department. Tell me about the girls you've gone out with. Any serious contenders?" She bites down on her finger again, and I can't help but feel like she's seducing me. Although something tells me she's not trying, it's just an aftereffect of being so damn beautiful. Hell, Izzy can seduce me simply by taking her next breath—already has.

"Let's see. I've had three relationships that have lasted longer than a few months. One of those lasted about a year, but the rest were revolving doors." More like revolving beds but I leave that part out.

"Sounds like you've been busy." She giggles into her words, and it's the first genuine smile I've gotten out of her all night. "I bet each of those girls wishes they had a second chance with you."

"Doubt it. How about you? How many broken hearts are you responsible for?" I know for a fact one—and that would be me all through high school. I moped for her every time I left the studio after picking up Annie. Deep down I think I still mope for Izzy. Hell, I know I do.

"None here. I'm a smooth operator." She gives a little wink. "I specialize in leaving them panting for more. God's honest truth right there."

Our food and drinks arrive, and she takes a quick sip of her water.

"Can I ask what your longest relationship was?" I'm not sure if I just entered a no-fly zone, but I'm betting her answer to this question is about to reveal more than I think.

"Ten years and counting." She tips her drink to me as if making a toast. "That would be with my cats. But they're loyal to a fault, and they know how to keep their paws to themselves—mostly."

"Very funny. Cats, huh? I'd like to meet them. Annie had a cat once. I think my dog ate it for breakfast one morning." I lean in and nudge my shoulder into hers. "I'm kidding. It took off for greener kitty pastures."

"You never know, I might be harboring it." She leans in further, and the light hits her just right, washing her olive skin smooth as velvet. My fingers tremble just wanting to touch her to confirm the theory. "I've got four strays."

"That's a lot of little mouths to feed. But I think you're evading the question. Longest relationship?" I'm getting the feeling Izzy is hiding something, and it's not just her relationship history. She's skittish. Something has her spooked, and it has for a while.

"Longest relationship." She glances down at the neat row of black-coiled dots in front of her. "How long have I known you?" She's teasing, but that hurt look in her eyes says she's not. "I don't do relationships, Holt. I don't think anyone's ever going to get that out of me." She stirs her drink with her straw, gazing off into the wall for a moment. "Besides, I want to stay close to my mom—make sure she's okay. I don't want her to be alone. No one should have to be alone."

"Does that include you?"

"Trust me, with Mom around, I won't be alone. Have I mentioned four cats?"

I glance down at my food, looks good, too bad my appetite took off about thirty seconds ago.

"What about, you know, having someone special in your life. Surely you'll need a man around to open up jars—give you a nice massage at the end of a long day at the studio." I meant for it to sound sarcastic, but, in truth, it sounded like some moronic question I'm insisting she answer.

"Mmm," she moans before swallowing her first bite. "The massage sounds heavenly. And, yes, a jar-opening man would be nice, but this is me we're talking about." She averts her eyes as if I should understand what it means. "I think I'll stick to psychotic blind dates for now. Baby steps, remember?"

"Got it." We take in the rest of our meal, sharing memories of West Hollow Brook High, her days as a cheerleader, the drama department. For someone who seemed so outgoing, she sure clammed up after high school.

Strange. Sounds like something big happened between then and now. And whatever it is, it still has a hold of her.

I plan on finding out exactly what it might be.

And then I'm going to free her.

At least I hope I can.

Ironic because, deep down, I know there's no one who could ever free me.

4

The Proposition

Izzy

Hi Dad,

I did it. I ventured into Laney's bear trap and had to spend an hour gnawing off my leg just to get away from the lunatic she paired me with.

Do you ever feel like life is trying to lead you in a direction you don't want to venture? And yet, ironically, I think I do want something along the same path. I'm just not sure it can ever fit into my life. Who could ever accept me when I can't seem to accept myself? Plus, I'm pretty sure shacking up with my mother isn't some poor boy's dream of a happily ever after. You know Mom. It would be more of a horror story. Funny, because without you, it's been nothing but a tragedy.

~Little Bit

ༀༀ

The rain drives down over Hollow Brook like axes being hurled from the sky as I run into the Black Bear with my jacket pulled over my head. It's the night of Laney and Ryder's engagement party which seems strange since they technically got engaged months ago, but, knowing my sister, it's her way of starting what she's affectionately dubbed her wedding season. It's officially the big countdown with only nine weeks to go. I went ahead and got fitted for a simple black dress, high collar, long sleeves. I'm not in the mood to attract attention to myself on Laney's big day or any other day to be exact. I've never wanted half the attention I've received. That scene from last night at the sushi bar runs through my mind. I could feel Holt probing. He wanted more, I could tell, but really the rest isn't all that important. I'm the reason my mother has had nothing but a string of revolving-door relationships. And, to be honest, I'm not holding my breath that things will work out with her and Greasy. Speaking of which.

Off at the far end of the bar, I spot my mother in a bright blue power suit. Her inky hair sits combed back neat with a matching blue bow plastered to the side of her head. She's laughing it up with a man about her age, well-dressed, gray hair, handsome. He seems nice enough. Too bad Greasy D is standing right beside her with his wandering eye while he levels the edge of a younger girl's miniskirt. Holt goes over and pats the gentleman on the back, joining their circle.

"Interesting," I whisper as I make my way in their direction.

An oversized banner is strung up over the bar, spelling out *Congratulations!* with little silver wedding bells dispersed throughout. A plethora of flowers sit on each table—white roses with a sprig of asparagus flowers thrown in for color. It looks beautiful and elegant, much like my baby sis. I couldn't be happier for her and Ryder.

"Hey there," I say as I step into the small circle, planting myself right next to Holt.

"Hey yourself." Holt gives an easy smile, and I feel right at home by his side.

"Marcus"—Mom pulls me in—"this is my daughter, Elizabeth. She's working on her spinstership with four cats currently under her charge. If you find a stray please give me a call because every cat lady worth her salt knows you can never have too many."

"Nice intro," I smart. "You can call me, Izzy," I say, accepting his hand as he gives a gentle shake. Spinstership. My mother keeps reminding me, that in three short years, I'll be turning thirty. You'd think I were inching my way toward a very steep cliff, and the only way to save myself from this horrible outcome is to strap myself to some poor, unsuspecting man for the rest of my life.

"Marcus Edwards," he says. I can't help but notice he looks slightly familiar—something about those glowing eyes. "This is my fiancé, Jenny." The girl by his side looks all of thirteen with her dark locks pulled into a sleek ponytail. Her over-bright lipstick gives her that playing-with-mommy's-makeup look.

"Izzy, this is my dad." Holt presses his hand into the small of my back, and I take a breath. I glance down at his arm, and he pulls it away, quick as it came.

I revert the attention back to his father and the ingénue he's linked himself with. "It's nice to meet you—both." God, is she really marrying him? No wonder my mother is stuck with men like Greasy D, all the good ones are busy trolling the sandbox for their next conquest. That can't be awkward *at all* for Holt, considering, legally, he'll be obligated to card his new stepmother for the next five years.

Mom fires up their conversation again, and Holt and I take a step back.

"Sorry about that." He glances down to my waist. "I wasn't trying to—"

I shake my head. "It was fine. If I want to date, I need to get used to things like that? Baby steps, right?"

He looks puzzled for a moment until the gravity of what I'm saying finally sinks in. It's my subtle way of letting him know I'm starting from scratch—that I have further to go than he could have ever imagined.

"Baby steps."

Bryson and Baya come up, and he gives his brother a friendly sock to the arm.

"What did I say about hitting on the patrons? Izzy is this bonehead bothering you?"

Baya swats her boyfriend over the arm. "Ignore him." She leans into me. "Holt is the second hottest guy in Hollow Brook. Isn't that right?" She gives a quick wink over to him.

"You're both funny." Holt shakes his head at his brother as if he were ready to gift him a new orifice.

"Who says he's second?" I tease.

Holt locks his gaze over mine with a sly smile building on his face. For a second it's just the two of us in the room, stealing a private moment.

Laney and Ryder breeze over. Her hair is up with a waterfall of curls rippling to the side. She's wearing a strapless mint green gown that finishes off that princess effect.

"Laney!" I give her a quick hug. "You look stunning." I pull back and take her in as tears blur my vision. Laney is beautiful and whole—normal in every way. I thank God every day she escaped our childhood untainted by the bullshit that went on behind the scenes. I did exactly what my father asked and made sure Laney was safe. I would have killed to protect her—almost did. Sometimes I wish I would have, although the fear of a prison sentence kept me from committing a felony. Ironic since here I am with my invisible bars, caging me in wherever I go.

Laney steps in and slings a perfumed arm over my shoulder. "Hey, you okay?"

"I'm fine." I look to Ryder. "I hope you know what a lucky guy you are. Don't even think of hurting my baby sister, or I'll have to hunt you down."

A light laugh rolls through our circle, but I meant every word.

"Let's do this." Bryson nods over at Ryder. They each take a hold of their respective girlfriends and navigate their way to the makeshift stage. Ryder picks up the mike, and a shrill of feedback whistles through the bar.

"Hello." He blows into it, and the room pops with the noise. "First, I want to thank each and every one of you for coming out tonight to celebrate this truly joyous occasion. I can't think of anything more important to me than joining with Laney in holy matrimony. The big day is just a few short weeks away, and I don't think we'll stop celebrating until we're old and gray." The crowd breaks out in a collective sigh. "There's another reason we called you here. Bryson and Baya, our good friends, have made a decision about their own big day. I'll hand the mike over to Bryson so he can let you in on that."

Holt looks to me a moment.

"You know anything about this?" I whisper.

"Not a clue. But I wondered what my parents were doing here. And I think I'm about to find out."

"Thank you, Ryder." Bryson takes a deep breath. "Baya has been a saving grace to me from the moment I met her. It wasn't long after that I figured out I couldn't live without her. As most of you know, we've been engaged now since February."

Baya leans into the mike. "Valentine's Day."

Another collective *aww* circles the room.

"And"—he picks up Baya's hand—"we've decided to tie the knot this summer as well."

Laney and Baya jump with excitement as if their heels were on springs. Here it comes.

"We've agreed that we're going to go ahead with a double wedding."

The room breaks out in cheers. An entire mob of people crash around them, and the music starts up overhead.

"Wow." I turn to Holt—"that's pretty wild. Your brother and my sister, same bat time, same bat channel."

"Who would have thought?" He forces a smile to come and go, but Holt looks sucker-punched far more than he does happy.

"Don't you like Baya?"

"Yes. Baya is perfect for my brother. Trust me, he test drove enough girls to confirm this theory." Holt's features darken as he gives a wistful smile. "It's just, he's cruising through life—I'm proud of him."

"And you're not cruising." I say it almost as an apology. "I get it."

"Looks like we're doing this baby steps thing together."

"Sounds good to me."

A slow song starts in, and an entire mob of couples drift toward the dance floor.

"You want to hit it?" Holt nods toward the lethargic moving crowd, and my entire body seizes.

"Just me and you?" I touch my hand to my chest to further confirm my stupidity.

"Well, we can ask your mom to join us, but it might get crowded." He tilts his head, and his lips curl in a seductive manner that make my insides disintegrate. "Yes, me and you." His lids hood low. "I won't bite. I promise."

"Not even if I ask real nice?" I press my lips in tight. I don't think I've ever felt so playful—so safe with anyone before.

His brows knit. "Only if you say please. How about it? You in, Princess?"

"Laney's the princess around here." I blow out a breath just looking at his expectant hand.

"I think 'kitten' fits you better anyway." We head over to the dance floor, and he weaves us deep into the crowd. His gaze never leaves mine, and I close my eyes a moment.

Holt slowly interlaces our fingers with his warm flesh rubbing over mine. Here it is, the contact I've craved for so long. A part of me was afraid it wouldn't feel right, that I would want to repel, but my insides are singing a song of their own, a sweet aching melody that drips right down to my thighs. I don't need a man around the house to open jars. It's moments like this I need him for. My mother flutters through my mind, and I'm quick to chase her away.

Holt glides his arm around my waist, and I let out a sigh that was ten years in the making.

"First slow dance?" He cocks his head just enough to make my bones melt.

I give a slight nod. Each time Holt asks a question, I feel as if I'm giving him another part of the puzzle. Too bad I'm missing a few pieces—the ones that fit over my heart. My father took those with him.

He leans in, and I groan as the warmth of his chest heats over mine.

Who knew Holt Edwards had the power to reduce me to cinder. I've danced plenty in my life—dancing *is* my life. But I've never done it with anybody else—at least not in this close proximity—with someone like Holt. Not once did I imagine it would feel like this—like a dream exploding into life, and here it is. I glance down at our legs touching in all the right places.

"Baby steps, kitten," he whispers with his hot breath raking over my neck.

I arch my head back and take in my fill, drink it down, savor it for later. This is it. My life has hit its zenith with Holt Edwards at the helm of this newfound revolution taking place inside me.

"Baby steps," I whisper.

I run my hand over his back, lower still until my arm wraps fully around his waist. My body loosens as if I had just untangled a knot I've been working on for a decade.

His cologne holds the scent of sandalwood and spices from the orient—something richer than the one he wore the first night.

"So you still up for giving this beginner a few pointers?" I offer his back a light scratch.

"You bet." Holt smolders into me as if he's ready to give me a whole lot more than I bargained for. "You did great at dinner. And you're killing the dance floor."

"So what's next?" I wet my lips without meaning to.

A tall, dark-haired guy, the one that Roxy introduced as her boyfriend the other day, pops up with his phone pointed at us. "Anything you'd like to say to the happy couples?"

"Not now, Cole." Holt spins us around, but his friend is Johnny on the spot with the camera pointed right at us again.

"Congratulations!" I sing into the small rectangle. "I wish you many happy years. You deserve it—all of you."

"Ditto," Holt snarls at his buddy and tells him to take off by way of hitching his head.

"What's the matter, Holty boy? You a little tongue tied?" Cole breaks out in a wicked grin. It's obvious he's enjoying the hell out of this. "I tell you what. I'm about to turn on the kiss cam for the night. Why don't you two kick us off?"

"No thanks." Holt pushes the camera away, but it's becoming quickly obvious Cole is committed to the cause. "Listen up, everybody! Any couple willing to smooch for the kiss cam tonight gets a drink on the house."

"That's coming out of your tips." Holt tries to turn us away from his friend's digital wrath, but Cole is stealth and right back in our face with his cell phone.

"First couple of the night," he bellows. "Will they or won't they?"

Oh shit. My heart seizes. My muscles cramp up. My entire body pulsates with a heartbeat of its own.

Slowly the bodies on the dance floor come to a stop, and, before I know it, half the bar is focused in on us.

"You in, kitten?" Holt looks sorry for me, hurt that I'd have to be subject to this at all.

I nod just once as if it were all my body could afford—probably is.

Holt leans in and whispers, "You don't have to do this. I own the bar. You can have any drink any time." He gives my hand a gentle squeeze, reassuring me of my newly minted booze on command status.

"Maybe I want to earn my drink like everybody else." Did those words just come out of my mouth? "I mean, you did say you'd be willing to teach me *everything*," I whisper. "I'm in."

It's as if a flare just went off straight through my skull, blowing out every self-imposed sanction I've ever given myself. A shiver rails through me, shaving me down to the bone at the prospect of kissing Holt right here in front of everyone. It feels dreamlike, like something that borders a nightmare, and you're not sure what direction it'll take.

My heart bangs in my chest as if it's trying to tap out. The floor starts to sway all on its own. There've been a few boys who have tried to sneak in a kiss over the years. Of course, each one of those episodes ended with me bolting. My legs start to shift as if preparing for the sprint to my car. I hike my shoulder up without thinking—affirming the fact I've still got my purse with me. I can always make up some lame excuse if my feet decide to carry me to the parking lot. It's worked before.

The crowd breaks out in a chant of *kiss, kiss, kiss*, and I can feel our heads magnetizing toward one another. Here it is. A moment I thought I never wanted, and yet, all of a sudden, I don't think I can live without.

My heart leaps into my throat, thrashing around like a fish out of water. My body explodes with the heat of a nuclear explosion. Holt's lids grow heavy until finally they close. He comes in until our lips brush over one another soft as melted butter, and a spasm of heat rips through me from head to toe.

An audible moan gets trapped in my chest as I lean in for more. Holt meets me right there as his lips move slowly over mine, warm, so incredibly cushioned. The crowd with their wild cheers—the music—the bar, it all fades to nothing as Holt gently pulls his lips over mine. Then the unthinkable happens. My mouth falls open, and I let him in. His teeth clash with mine. His tongue comes to me with a gentle sweep at first then an all out aggression as it mingles with mine. My stomach explodes with a thousand butterflies with wings of fire, and the flames sear right down to my feet.

This is my moment—our moment, and I wish nothing more than for the dance floor to swallow us whole so we can be alone, doing just this, surrendering to one another for the rest of time immemorial. Holt and I are teetering on my own personal oblivion, staring down each one of my demons in the face. This, right here, is where the old me ends and the new me begins—with Holt Edwards—with his gentle persuasive kisses, I think I can cross the threshold and make it to the other side.

Mostly.

Holt

Holy shit.

Here it is. The summer I've waited for my entire life.

My insides grind. Ready or not, I'm coming to life in my boxers. For what it's worth, I'm struggling to keep it together. It's so easy to buy into the fact this is just another wet dream starring Izzy Sawyer. There's no way I'm publically making out with Izzy during waking hours right here at the bar.

Her tongue moves over mine, smooth and slow. For as much as she's hinted she's new at all this, she's pretty damn good at what she's doing. Kissing Izzy is like falling into a warm lake at midnight. It's paradise, bliss, one erotic second after the other.

"*Hey.*" Bryson comes up from behind. "Your parents are here, so is her mom. Keep it G, dude." He walks on by as if he never said a word.

I pull back and take her in. Her lips are rosy, her cheeks flushed, and she's looking up at me with a dreamy look in her eye. At least that's what my ego is feeding me.

"You okay?" I'm half afraid she'll slap me straight and run for the exit.

"I'm fine." She shakes her head as if coming out of a trance. "Wow." Her gaze falls to her feet. "Thank you for that."

"Thank *you*." I raise my brows. "I believe I owe you a drink. Whiskey?"

"Only the best." She gives a quick wink. "But I'm driving, so I'll take a rain check."

The music picks up pace, and the dance floor swarms with a small army of girls spontaneously kicking off their heels. Laney bumps her hip into Izzy.

"Podiatrist." She glares at her sister a moment before offering me a dry smile. I've seen that look on Laney's face enough to know she's more than a little pissed.

"Podiatrist?"

"It's my Wednesday night fright." Her shoulders hike to her ears. The light shines from her lips, and I want to kiss it off. "The next date on the list."

The thought of Izzy going out on a date with anyone but me fills my stomach with battery acid.

"Sounds like you might need a little more practice to help get things off on the right foot." Shit. Did I just say that? What I should have said was forget the foot doctor, and let me take you somewhere so we can replicate that kiss over and over.

"Practice, huh?" Her body tenses against mine as she holds back a laugh.

Great. Make her think that kiss was anything less than stellar.

"No, that's not right. You've got it down, Iz," I whisper so low I'm not sure she heard. "You're perfect." She takes a breath as her body presses against my chest.

She looks up, and, for one glorious second, I think she's gunning for another kiss. Izzy takes a full step back and irons out her jeans with her hands. I reel her back in by the fingers. "If you want that whiskey, you can come to my place anytime. I serve it with grilled cheese and a smile just so you know what you're getting yourself into, kitten."

She swallows hard. "Maybe I will. And maybe you can help me work on my lip-lock. I think you're right. I'm a little rusty."

I shake my head. "You're not rusty." Izzy can give pointers to every girl I've ever been with. That might have been her first kiss in a while, but what she was offering was miles ahead of the game compared to anything I've ever received. Izzy's kiss, much like the rest of her, is sheer perfection. "But I'm not one to turn a person away when they're in need of help." I hold back the goofy grin trying to etch itself over my face. Just the thought of tasting those lips again has my body begging to defy gravity.

"You're a good friend." Her eyes widen when she says that last word.

Friend.

And there it is. That's all Izzy wants with me—a friendship. But I'm getting the feeling that's all she wants with anyone. Ironic since that's me in a nutshell.

Annie bounces over and signs to me.

"She says my parents want to speak with me for a minute."

"No problem. I'd better head home before my cats think I've abandoned them. If I'm gone too long they have a tendency to drown my nightie in their water bowl."

"Sounds like they enjoy seeing you naked." Crap.

That's right. Show her you have no filter, and see how many months go by without seeing her again. It was five last time. Not that she was running from me, but that didn't stop me from counting the hours.

"Naked?" Izzy belts out a laugh and her teeth glitter in turn. "I guess they're typical boys." She touches her hand to my cheek and holds it there a moment. "Good night, Holt." I watch as she sways her hips all the way out the door, and my heart breaks because every last part of me wishes I were going with her.

⚜

Annie leads me to the back where we have a table and chairs set out for employee breaks. Mom sits off to the side with a decidedly ticked-off expression, and I can't say I blame her. Jenny is seated square on my dad's knees, giving him what looks like the lap dance of the century while my father holds her at the hips.

I slap Bryson some skin. "Congrats, bro."

"You up for best man?" He pulls me into a half hug.

"You bet." That almost guarantees I'll get to dance with Izzy again, and this time I can't help the goofy grin from blooming on my face.

"So you and Sawyer, huh?" He shakes his head as if scolding me on some level. "Is it the real deal?"

I glance over to Mom who looks far more lonely than she ever has before, and it both pisses me off and breaks my heart.

"Nah, Iz and I are just friends." For a second there I almost forgot I destroy relationships, not build them. Regardless, Izzy's not up for some traditional relationship, at least not with me. I guess we'll see how things pan out with the foot doctor on Wednesday. In fact, I think I'll add myself to the schedule that night so I can see firsthand where this goes. "So what's up?"

I pull a seat out for Annie, and she takes it.

Dad clears his throat. "I've come to a rather sad conclusion." He glances at my mother then to Bryson and me. "I'll be putting the bars up on the market."

"What?" Bryson is shocked as shit for the both of us.

"Its simply time. They've had a good run, but my head's no longer in it." He pats his girlfriend on the knee to let us know exactly where his little head is at. "There's no point in going forward. This was once a joint venture between your mother and I, and I've held onto them longer than I needed to. I've already agreed to help pay half of Annie's education. And, Bryson, I'll do the same for you until you finish up with your masters, but that's all she wrote. The bars—much like your mother and I—are history."

My fist glides over my palm just hearing him talk about her that way. She gave him everything, and he's just

98

sitting there grinding his heel into what they once had. I hate him—I hate *me* for this.

"So what's next?" I ask as if I didn't know. I get the ax, *that's* what's next.

"I'm going to work it out with the new owner to keep the staff, at least for a little while. And, whatever you do, I wouldn't tell anyone just yet. Trust me, you'll have a mutiny by morning if people think they'll be losing their jobs. I don't want to spook anyone." He gets up and wraps an arm around his new gal pal as if it were perfectly normal, and I'm afraid that's exactly what it is—the new normal.

They take off, and Bryson gives me a light sock to the arm.

"You all right, man?"

"I'm great. Just a little caught off guard."

Mom comes over and gives us each a hug. "Don't worry. It'll all work out I promise."

I nod as if I believed it, but, the truth is, nothing is going to work out. I'm about to lose the one thing I had that was real in my life, this damn piece of real estate.

Bryson has Baya and his shiny new degree. Annie has a bright future which starts in a few short weeks at Whitney Briggs. And what do I have? A front row seat as the girl of my dreams dates a podiatrist. Nothing more.

That kiss from earlier comes back strong, and a surge of adrenaline spikes through me, vying for hope.

There's something more brewing between Izzy and me.

I can feel it, and judging by that kiss, so can she.

5

Touching You, Touching Me

Izzy

Dad,

Every now and again I get thrown for a loop. I've worked so hard to build this fort around me, and sometimes I get tired of holding up the walls. It's so damn heavy. Sometimes I just want to be normal. Is there such a thing?

Confused,
~Iz

છુૠજી

Wednesday morning, the sun splits through a crack in the curtains and blinds me with its overbearing exuberance. It's not that I can't appreciate a nice sunny day, but I happened to be enjoying where my mind had wandered off to and sort of wanted to linger. I haven't had a dream like that in, well, never. I was at Holt's apartment, and we were in the middle of a mad video game session just laughing our asses off, staring at the screen, neither one of us willing to lose. Something about the whole scene, about being with Holt and just having a good time with him made me happy.

A tail lashes over my face and tickles my nose.

"Sneezy." I push him away and accidentally slide him right off the bed. "Oops, sorry."

That dream felt so real. It felt good, comfortable hanging out with Holt like that. Usually I'm repelled by men, and, yet, with Holt it's like I can't get enough.

I stumble out of bed and into the living room. There's so much to do before next Thursday, the big twenty-year anniversary of the studio. And it's been twice as stressful since I'm planning a few surprises for my mother. It's impossible to keep anything from her.

The cats congregate around my ankles with their good morning wails, tripping me twice on the way to the kitchen. The strong smell of cigarette smoke comes from the living room, and I head in that direction.

"Would you knock that off?" I burst in to find Greasy D lying on the couch with one hand down his pants and the TV on low. "We don't smoke." Or masturbate in open areas of the house, but I leave that part out for now.

"Well, darlin'—I do." He takes a hit and blows a mini tornado from his thin, greasy lips. His gray hair is sticking straight up, what little he has left, and his stubble looks as if his face has been sprayed with silver shards.

"Mom?" My voice escalates in horror. If anything she'll go batshit when she sees he's lit one up, and that alone will be worth the show.

"She ain't here. She was up early and out the door while your lazy ass was sawing logs."

"And what exactly is it that your lazy ass does?" I'm so pissed. I'm shaking. Usually I don't mean to chase away my mother's boyfriends, it sort of happens by default, but this is one I'd like to missile launch into space.

"I'm looking after you." He gives a quick wink and rides his stoned-out eyes over my tank top and shorts in a tactile manner. I can feel those invisible hands roving over me as I cry out for my mother all those years ago. Instinctually I cover my chest and head for the kitchen. I think it's time to have a talk with Mom. I don't know why the hell she'd want a moron like Greasy D in her life.

And why is she such a magnet for creeps, anyway?

⁂❦

The studio has a few extra cars in the lot, and I know for a fact one of them belongs to my sweet baby sis. It's odd since Laney hasn't been here in ages.

I head in and say a quick hello to Bella, the girl who has worked behind the front desk for the last five years. She was the first person I hired when I took the reins from my mother. Well, not officially. Mom runs a tight ship, but she graciously handed over a majority of the grunt work once I began working here fulltime. The only duty she's held onto was the books, and, truthfully, money management has never been my forte as evidenced by my under-the-mattress method of personal banking.

"Izzy?" Laney comes up from the hall and gives me a quick hug.

"Fancy meeting you here." I mean it. "Considering it as a venue for the reception?"

There's no way in hell Laney would even dream of the idea. She's always had champagne taste, and, lucky for her, because Ryder can build an entire house out of Dom Perignon bottles if he wanted. Speaking of dreams, Holt pops back into my mind.

"Right." She nods into me. "And we'll have the buffet laid out right here at the sign in desk." She makes a face at poor Bella who's inundated with the phone ringing off the hook.

"Let's head in." I lead us to the studio where, shockingly, Mom is speaking to a group of irate mothers. What is this, bring your family to work week? Although, technically, I didn't bring either of them. The mothers start in with their bickering. "Sometimes I think we should initiate a drop-off rule," I whisper to Laney. "That would cut back on ninety percent of the drama that takes place around here."

"Yeah, well, Mom can work on her delivery a little. I'm sure that would cut back on eighty."

"Touché." I walk her back to my office where the shelves are lined with all of my favorite dance magazines. I remember when Laney and I used to pour over them for hours. But, then, my mother deemed Laney unworthy of the studio, and she's never quite recovered from that. In my mother's defense, Laney was heard on multiple occasions saying she had a spot on the team because her mother owned the place. She outright refused to come to practice most days. "So—what brings you here?"

"Mom mentioned that the studio was turning twenty, and I wanted to see if there was something I could do to help. Roxy says she's bringing cupcakes."

"And I can't wait to sink my teeth into them. As for the celebration, I've got it handled. I'm sending out fliers today with each of the girls, and I'm going to have the lead team work on a banner. I'm having everyone at the studio sign it. I thought it'd be a nice memento for Mom."

"You're right, it will be." She sits on the edge of my desk. Laney has let her hair grow out long, and now it's nearly the same length as mine. We look enough alike that we could be fraternal twins ourselves minus the fact we're five years apart. She looks at me sideways. "You're always looking out for Mom." She strums her nails over the desk, filled with suspicion. "Is everything okay?"

"Yes. Why wouldn't it be?"

"I don't know. It's just that comment Jemma made the other night about me not knowing you—it got me thinking. She said it would take more than 'the one' to set your heart straight. Is something going on? If there's something happening, I'd like to be let in on the big secret." She leans in as her features soften. "I'm your sister, Iz, and, to be honest, the more I thought about it, the more it hurt to think you might be sharing something with Jemma instead of me."

And there it is. Laney knows I'm holding something back. My blood turns to ice at the thought of telling her what Jemma knows.

I give a brief smile holding up a stack of mail. "I'd chat all day, but I need to pare down this stack before my first class. Speaking of busy, is there anything I can do to help out with the big day? I'm really good at running errands."

"Bills? My *wedding*? Wow"—she sinks into the seat across from me—"this must be big. So what is it? You have some rap sheet I don't know about?"

"Maybe. Or maybe I want to keep my pole-dancing career to myself for a while. Anyway, it's none of your business. And did you see that I got fitted for my bridesmaid dress?"

"Yes. Thank you. And since we're on the subject of being sneaky just know that Morticia Addams getup you ordered has been changed out for something more modern that I would be proud to have at my wedding. Are you running a funeral home on the side? Because it all makes sense now."

I give a hard blink. "I get it—it's your wedding." The thought of wearing something Laney picked out for me makes me cringe. "You win. Unfortunately, I wasn't kidding about the bills." I pretend to bury my nose in a costume catalog. Just the thought of Laney not letting this go makes me sick.

She gets up and heads for the door. "Tonight at seven—the Black Bear. Be there."

"Can't wait to meet my future podiatrist."

"He's the one, Iz, I can feel it." Her shoulders hike to her ears with excitement. "I can't wait for you to have what Ryder and I do. Hey, I know, if you guys really hit it off, maybe we can double date sometime? It's always been a dream of mine to have a double date with my big sis." She hugs the doorframe and swoons. "I'd do anything to see you happy, Iz."

"I know."

Laney takes off, and I lean back in my seat.

I'd do anything to see her happy, too.

And I did.

∞∞

The Black Bear is congested with a flood of amped up girls in extra short skirts and tops that barely cover the northern hemisphere.

Holt's cologne calls to me, and I scan the bar, but there's no sign of him.

Baya waves as I step inside, so I go over.

"What gives?" I ask, following her to the back. "Free beer night?"

"More like open mike night." She holds out a seat for me, and I take it—same dark, distal corner as the last disaster. I'm guessing Laney thinks it's romantic to tuck me away in no man's land with the next maniac on her list. "We're auditioning for a house band. If the boys like 'em, they can get a recurring gig. It's something Bryson and Holt have been wanting to do for a while."

"Nice. A sexy bass player equals lots of revenue from half dressed coeds. Sounds like win-win."

"Speaking of win"—Baya takes a seat—"I saw that kiss the other night." She leans in with her eyes bulging like a pair of hardboiled eggs. "Are you sure you need Laney's dating service? Looks to me like you're doing just fine on your own."

I glance at the bar and spot Holt tending to a group of smitten girls at least six years my junior. One of them is Marley, Jemma's baby sister. Crap. Just looking at the way she's fawning over him makes me sick to my stomach. Marley is cute and young and the exact kind of girl someone like Holt should end up with. Not the walking bag of issues I've become.

"I'm not really on the relationship track right now." Heat floods to my cheeks as I think about that kiss, about that dream I had last night. If I *was* into relationships I know exactly where I'd look first. "Anyway, Holt can have whatever girl he wants, and, by the way, I qualify to be his much older sister. We're just friends. Really, it's no big deal."

"Who says age even matters? Did you see the cradle robbing that Edwards senior is partaking in? Emphasis on *senior*. I'm telling you, that man has socks that are older than 'Jenny.'"

A dull laugh pumps through me. "Yeah, but he's a man."

"So? Break the double standard." Baya strums her candy pink nails over the table. "If a man can date someone younger so can a woman."

"Look"—I take in Baya with her perfect hair and flawless complexion—"I'm not really into making new inroads for women's lib and for darn sure I don't want to be the poster child for cougars the world over."

"Chill out, Izzy. You're not that much older than him." She reaches over and touches her hand to mine. "I get it. It's not the norm, so it feels weird. If it's any consolation, my mom had three years on my dad, and they had one hell of a marriage."

"Still going strong?"

She sags in her seat. "My dad passed away when I was in junior high." She inverts her lips as if holding back tears. "But I know for a fact my mom is glad she didn't let a little thing like their age difference stop her from the best relationship she's ever had. My brother and I are kind of glad, too." She reaches over and gives me a brief hug. "You'll figure it out." She looks past my shoulder and frowns. "Here we go. Have fun on your date, Iz."

Baya takes off, and Laney appears in her place. Next to her is a seemingly normal, rather nice looking man—

who could be my father. And there's that. I guess my ageism runs in both directions.

"Cliff Lancaster." He extends his hand, and I gently shake it.

"*Dr.* Cliff Lancaster," Laney whispers with excitement. God, does she really see me with this guy? It's obvious Laney can't see past the M.D. in his name to properly observe the fact he's old enough to be our father. And why do I suddenly feel like introducing myself as Jenny?

"Izzy," I say it forced in the event my tongue decides to take a U-turn without my permission.

"How about a tall cold one, Dr. Lancaster?" Laney pulls his seat out as if he were a girl. Geez. Note to self, trip Laney for the hell of it tonight, preferably while she's holding a tray full of *cold ones*. "And a daiquiri for you?"

I nod and wave her off.

"So tell me something about yourself." He gives a pleasant smile, and suddenly I feel like an ass for being so aggressively judgmental. I mean, just because he's got a head full of gray hair, and matching hairy knuckles, doesn't mean he's incapable of holding an intelligent conversation. Why do I get the feeling a running commentary of a political nature is about to ensue? Again with the ageism.

"I run my mother's dance studio. Oh, and I love cats."

"The musical?" His brows peak, and it's only then I notice an entire rash of liver spots running down his left cheek. I quickly glance away and try to focus in on his smile. He sure has a nice set of pearly whites. A visual of him taking them out at night and slipping them in a glass runs through my mind.

I blink to attention. "The musical? No—no." I give a nervous laugh. "The furry creatures. I have four."

"Well." The smile glides right off his face. "I'm allergic, but I can make an exception for someone as stunning as yourself." He reaches over and cups his hand over mine. And eww? Why do I feel like I'm sitting on my mother's couch while one of her geriatric boy toys hit on me? A flashback of that night slaps me in the face, and I'm quick to withdraw my fingers.

"Tell me something about you." I slip my hands into my lap where I plan on keeping them for the next fifteen minutes. That's exactly how long I predict I'll have to sit here—what with the family emergency that's about to occur. I glare over at Laney at the far end of the bar. It's going to be very fucking tragic. A hospitalization might be involved.

"I'm a foot doctor. My job stinks, and so do my patients." He barks out a laugh, exposing two neat rows of perfectly capped teeth. At least he's got a nice smile, although the sense of humor is debatable. "I hear they've got a full menu here." He peruses the offerings. "You care to grab a bite?"

I sort of like the fact he's interested in feeding me even if it does scream paternal.

"Yes. For sure."

"I've already had dinner, how about we skip to dessert?" His brows dip down, and I can't help note the sexual connotation he's just inferred. Am I dessert?

"That's fine. I hear they've got a great tiramisu."

He bleeds a lewd smile, and I'm quick to eye the exit.

Crap. Laney needs to see an optometrist *and* a psychologist. And now I'm beginning to wonder if there's more to Ryder than meets the eye. Where the hell did she get her idea of acceptable men? My mother?

Laney bops over, and we put in our orders.

"Anything else I can get you two?" She says it low and husky, and it's all I can do not to shove her into the next table.

"That should be it." I flat line. I'll deal with her later.

"Izzy"—he tips his chin up and looks at me in that physician-set-for-retirement sort of way—"I see you're wearing ballerina flats. Do you mind taking off your shoes? I'm a good judge of character based on foot care alone."

Did he just cop to the fact he's going to judge me solely on the condition of my hooves?

I do a quick sweep for Laney. This has got to be a joke.

"I suppose." I mean, really? What's the worst that can happen? He finds a planter wart and runs out the door? At this point I'd welcome an entire host of pathogens so long as they get me and my toenails out from the scrutiny of the good doctor.

I flick off both shoes and point my feet in his direction.

"Oh, my." His mouth falls open as he leans over to inspect them. Without warning both feet are in his lap, and I'm quick to grab the lip of my seat in an effort to maintain my balance.

Holy hell. I try extracting my ankles from his stranglehold, but he's got a death grip.

"Quite the fine specimens if I do say so myself." His chest heaves over and over as if he's just ran around the bar with his pants on fire. He clasps his hand over my right foot and closes his eyes, clearly losing himself in a sexual euphoria I want no part of.

"Nice." I pluck myself free from his unwanted vice and dig my feet back into my shoes.

"It was more than nice." He leans in. His features distort with a look of ecstasy. "And, if you like—there's more where that came from."

That's exactly what I'm afraid of.

Laney reappears with a tiramisu for each of us and plunks down two steaming mugs of coffee.

"The java's on the house." She gives a little wink before taking off.

Honest to God. We're going to have to work on code words if she insists on pulling off these shenanigans. Like Coke Head or Foot Fetish.

He bears into me, leaning across the table as if he's going to keel over at any moment. God, maybe he's having a heart attack? Or he's falling into a sugar coma? Personally, I'm rooting for the cardiac episode.

"You know what I'd like to do with this?" His brows invert giving him a slightly demented look.

Holy hell. Do I want to know?

"Inhale it all in just one bite?" A blocked windpipe on his part will do quite nicely.

He picks up his plate and places it carefully on the floor.

What's he doing? Is there a small animal roaming the floor that I haven't noticed? Is he trying to say the food is bad?

He leans forward and produces his wallet from his ass, and I'm slow to follow the direction this is heading.

He pulls out a bill just enough for me to see that it's a Benjamin. "I'm willing to give you one hundred dollars if you dip your foot into that dessert."

"Why would I do that?" I'm confused. Is that some social norm I'm not privy to that gives the establishment you're eating at the big *F you*? God, I really have to get out more. If this is the case, society is experiencing a serious case of devolution, and soon we'll all be right back to thinking the earth is flat.

His lips twitch with a smile. "So I can watch."

Watch?

"What?" I jump back in my seat. Okay, I have to give it to him. I did not see that coming. I'm guessing the demented doctor can keep me entertained all night with his fetish requests and touchy feely fingers. In truth, I'm fearing for more than my piggies.

"Go ahead." He tosses me the bill, and it lands square on the whipped top layer of my yummy Italian treat. Great, now he's defiled both our desserts.

I glance up at the bar and spot Holt looking in this direction.

"I've gotta go. There's a man at the bar that needs me." I snatch the bill off my plate and run like hell.

I bet he didn't know I charge fifty bucks a piece to feel my feet.

Freaky bastard.

Holt

Izzy flies over, and the idiot Laney paired her with ditches out the side exit.

"What happened? Did he touch you?"

"Yes, he touched me."

Fuck. I jump the counter and land next to her.

"You okay? You need me to break some kneecaps?"

"Yes." She touches her hands to her temples. "I mean no. No breaking of the kneecaps. I'm fine. Let's just say he was overtly interested in what I'm hiding in my shoes."

Laney pops up with a ticked off look on her face. "What the hell? I just saw Dr. Lancaster run out of here like a fugitive. Did you say something to him?"

"No." She holds up a hundred dollar bill and grins. "I stole his money. He said he'd pay me to plunge my foot in his dessert. He's a sicko, Laney. Are you happy now? You're two for two."

Laney claps her hand over her mouth. "God, I'm so sorry! I swear I'll make sure to thoroughly investigate the next guy I throw your way. You're not mad are you?" She shrinks a little when she says it.

"No. I'm not mad." Izzy takes a seat and glares down at her shoes as if she'd like to burn them. "How about we cap the age limit at fifty? And I don't mind broke just as long as he's not homeless or allergic to cats. And please no illegal addictions or fetishes."

"Got it." Laney strokes her sister's hair. "I've got to finish up my shift. I'll catch up with you Thursday at the party for ELDS?"

"Deal."

Laney takes off, and Iz looks at me from under her lashes.

"I've got a hundred bucks. You up for dinner?"

I toss my dishtowel to Cole. "It looks like you've scored your second date for the evening. Anywhere you want to go?"

"How about Chinese take-out at your place?"

"Sounds perfect."

"You wouldn't happen to have any video games would you?"

"Are you kidding? I've got a library that puts the Game Hut to shame."

We head out the door and into the brisk night air— just Izzy and me. The way it's supposed to be.

ജാ

Iz follows me over to the apartment in her car. I've already called in the food, and the delivery guy shows up right as we hit the door.

"Good timing." I pull out my wallet, but Izzy insists on paying. No matter how hard I protest she covers the bill.

"I owe you dinner," I say as we get the food and head on in. "Somewhere nice—other than here."

"I'm good with here."

"So, you want to talk about tonight's misadventure?"

"I'd rather not." She taps the sofa. "You mind?"

"Go right ahead." I start up a fire before landing myself next to her. We divvy up the boxes and dive right in with our plastic flatware, our fortune cookies already on the floor.

"Sorry about pulling you away from the bar." She bows into her food and bats those long, dark lashes in my direction.

Hell, I'd give up the bars to be here with Izzy, not that my father didn't already beat me to the punch.

"You didn't. I volunteered."

"I dreamed about you last night." Her cheeks darken with color.

Hot damn. Izzy just said the words I never knew I wanted to hear.

"I guess that makes me the man of your dreams, kitten. Was it PG?" I dig my fork in my noodles trying not to let onto the fact my balls just incited a riot.

"It was very much PG." She tilts her head at the thought of me implying it was anything but. "We were playing video games. I beat you, by the way."

"Did you?" I set my plate down on the coffee table and fire up the tube. "I've got a hundred bucks that says you won't."

"I accept. But be warned, I'm on a roll. Hundred dollar bills are practically flying into my hands tonight."

"Game on." I flip a controller her way and dig another one out from under the couch. "Zombie Assault. I'll make things easy on you and go for best out of five."

"Easy on me, huh?" Her brows peak into her smooth forehead. Her milk-white teeth graze over her lips in amusement.

I offer a brief rundown of the rules, and we go at it for the next hour and a half.

"Fuck," I mutter as I watch myself get eaten by yet another member of the undead. "You're pretty good at this."

"Who knew?" Izzy places her controller on the coffee table, and I do the same. "That was fun. You make me feel good, Holt. Before I was just existing, but now I'm living. Every part of me feels alive around you." She clamps her lips shut tight as if the words slipped out without her permission. "I'd better get going." Her lids lower as she eyes the door, but her body is slow to get with the idea.

"You got another hot date?" I hold back a grin. "Maybe a chiropractor this time? Someone ready and willing to jump on your back for a while?"

She belts out a laugh, arching her long, pale neck, and it takes everything in me not to lean in and kiss it. Izzy is a work of art that's come to life. I've always thought so, but on a night like tonight when she's just inches away, it makes me want to verify it by way of my mouth.

"You wish." She leans back and closes her eyes a moment. "Come to think of it, a man who knows how to ease the tension in my aching muscles doesn't sound like such a bad idea."

Crap.

"I can do that," I offer.

Her eyes spring open.

"I give a mean massage." I might be lying, but, just in case I'm not, I threw it out there.

Her mouth falls open. That smile she's been wearing all night glides right off. Her chest rises and falls as her gaze meets up with mine.

"Let's see what you've got, cowboy." Her eyes hook into mine. We stay that way for a minute without a breath exchanged between us.

"You sure?"

"Yes." She perks to life, adjusting her back to me, and pulling her hair to the side.

I place my hands over her shoulders and soak in the sensation. A current travels up my arms as I close my eyes and memorize the feeling. Izzy is warm and soft and everything I thought she would be. I start in slow, digging my fingers into her flesh ever so gently, and she sways, moaning as I increase the effort. I'm willing to bet every hundred dollar bill I've got on the fact this is Izzy's first massage, and I guess that covers whether or not she's a virgin. I shake my head at the idea. There's no way. She's too damn sweet and gorgeous to have held out this long. Not that I plan on asking for confirmation. That's one conversation I don't dare initiate with her. But if it's true, I'm curious as to why. For sure it's not something I would have guessed a few weeks ago. Maybe she's saving it for the wedding night?

"You ever think of getting married someday?" I whisper right over her ear, and both of us freeze. Shit. Really? No fucking filter.

She turns her head. "Are you proposing?"

"Only if you're about to say yes."

She laughs, and her back bounces. "How about I take a rain check. I haven't quite mastered the fine art of dating. I think I should cross one relationship threshold at a time."

Can't pretend like I'm not happy about the rain check.

"How about you?" She turns the question around. "Do you hear wedding bells in the not-so-distant future?"

"I don't know about that." I took away the chime from my parent's marriage, so I'm pretty sure that disqualifies me from a happily ever after of my own or at least it should. "Maybe I'll just wait for you to say yes."

Her back bounces once again with a laugh. Izzy turns around, pressing those watery blue eyes into mine.

"I'll tell you a secret if you tell me one."

My heart stops. Maybe this is it. Maybe she's about to unleash what's been eating at her all these years.

I lean in until I can feel her breath on my face, warm and sweet like afternoon sunshine.

"Shoot."

"I'm not cut out for relationships, Holt." Her lips press together. She tears up, ready to lose it. I watch as my reflection wobbles in both her beautiful eyes, and it makes me want to cry like a pussy myself. "I'm not even close to going there."

"Me either." The briefest smile plays on my lips.

A beat of silence thumps by.

"Looks like we're on the same page."

"Looks like we are." I push in closer until our lips are less than an inch apart.

"But just in case." Her tongue does a quick revolution over her lips. "You think you can teach me a few tricks? I mean if things ever get physical, I'm not sure I'd know what to do." She eyes my mouth, and I can't help but smile.

I close my eyes and brush my lips over hers ever so softly. "Like that?"

"I was thinking more like this." Izzy dives over my mouth as if she's wanted a bite out of me all night long. But, the truth is, I'm the one who's been craving her—for as long as I can remember.

Izzy tastes like sugar, so achingly sweet I never want this moment to end. I wrap my arms around her waist and gently pull her closer without ever breaking our stride. Izzy delivers moan after moan, straight down my throat, and I return the favor with longer, stronger groans. Her hands find my waist. Her fingers ride up my shirt, carefully padding along my chest. Izzy moves in slow, easy strides as she explores the landscape. If this were any other girl, I would have long since returned the favor. I'd have both our clothes off, and I'd be ravaging her by now. But this isn't any other girl. This is Iz. And, if these are the baby steps she needs, I want to be right here to give them to her. In fact, I can stay on this step all night—all year if she wants.

"Holt." She pulls away just enough to take me in. "I hope you don't think I'm using you."

My chest bucks with a quiet laugh. "I promise." I raise a hand in the air. "It never crossed my mind." I comb my fingers through her hair. "Do you think I'm taking advantage of you?"

"What? *No*." She taps her hand over my chest. "I think we're just really friendly around one another." She bites down on her lip. Her features sag for a moment. "And I think you're beyond nice to put up with a basket case like me."

"Basket case? What makes you think so?" I'm hoping she'll take the bait.

She blows out a breath and traces circles over my chest. "I'm not sure I'm ready to go there."

Progress. The first step to solving a problem is admitting you have one.

"But I might." She scoots into me until her chest lays soft over mine. "You make me feel safe, and I can't thank you enough for that."

"I'm glad." I bury a kiss in her hair.

"Now getting back to what we were doing." She pulls her hand from my shirt and touches a line down my nose to my lips. "I think I'll need all the pointers you're willing to offer."

"Sounds like we'd better get busy."

"We'd better," she whispers, pressing her lips to mine.

Izzy and I start in on a viral assault, exploding into one another's mouths like solar flares, hard and rushed as if time were running out for the two of us. This is the stuff that dreams are made of. Izzy is definitely the girl of my dreams.

I wonder what has her thinking she's such a "basket case." Doesn't she know I'm the only basket case around here?

I wonder if the two of us could ever work.

Maybe all two broken people really need are each other.

6

Dance Hall Days

Izzy

Dad,

I did it. I took a step in a direction that I never thought I would go in, and I liked it. I can't tell you how long I've wondered if I would ever cross that threshold. So much was holding me back. Deep down, I was afraid something like that would never happen. I guess what I'm trying to say is that I'm ready to break some boundaries I thought I'd never cross. Okay, this is drifting into the weird zone, so I'll sign off for now.

Do me a favor and show up sometime, would you? I would appreciate the hell out of it. Or at least I think I would. I'm not sure I could ever really be mad at you. I probably should be, so if you ever do come back, wear armor.

Love you—mostly,
~Izzy

ഇരു

Any morning you wake up with a mouthful of fur is guaranteed to be a bitch from eyelids open.

I rush through my routine and run around my room like a spaz trying to find my purse before remembering I left it in the kitchen last night.

"I'm late," I mutter as I struggle to put on my shoes while hopping down the hall. No time for breakfast. I'll hit Starbucks on my way to the—

I spot my purse on the table, unzipped and splayed out. Funny. I don't remember leaving it like that. I head over and pluck out my wallet and find that too unzipped. Now I for damn sure know I wouldn't leave it like that. I peer inside only to find it empty. Crap. I had forty-five dollars left from Mr. Let-Me-Sniff-Your-Feet, and now it's up and disappeared.

"Donny?"

A groan comes from the living room. I stagger over in a blind rage and bump into the moron himself.

"Did you take money out of my wallet?" At this point it's a bit of a rhetorical question.

His hair is rumpled, his eyes half closed. He doesn't say a word, a sure sign of guilt in the first degree.

God. What is it with my mother and idiots? Does she require they come with some pedigree that specifically dictates they've been inbred? Must they be derelict fugitives to gain entry into her bedroom?

"Okay, look. I'm going to be really nice about this."
Lie number one. "Give it back, and I'll forget it ever
happened." Lie number two. "And I'll never mention it to
my mother." Lie number three—the most delicious of
them all.

"Can't." His breath blasts over me, thick with vodka.
"Spent it."

Gah! "I can't believe you're not even trying to cover
it up!"

"Take it easy. It's bad enough I had to hear your
mother yapping all night about some big celebration down
at that dance club you pretend to run. I had to do
something. If it makes you feel better, I can tell her the
flowers were from the both of us."

Flowers? He blew my hard-earned foot fondling
money on dying roses? That's about as nonsensical as
liquor at this point.

"You owe me forty-five dollars." I try to step around
him, but he blocks my path.

His eyes steady over my body, probing with his gaze
as tactile as if he were feeling me up with his fingers. "You
up for earning it back?"

"You wish." That's it. He's history. "Get out of my
way." I bolt around him just as he slaps me over the ass.
"Get *out* you asshole! Get out before I come home, or the
next thing you'll find in my purse will be your balls!" My
voice knifes through the morning air with the promise of a
dull razor. "And don't ever come back!"

I run all the way to the car and lock myself inside. My heart plows up into my throat. A cold sweat erupts all over my body.

"Shit." I pant as I start up the car.

Forty-five bucks says he'll be out by nightfall.

And then my mother will be alone again.

It's always because of me.

And not once have I ever regretted it.

⚭

The dance studio buzzes all day with the pre-party hype. Roxy shows up with far more cupcakes than I ever imagined.

"They look and smell glorious." I moan over the pink confections, and an image of Holt and his searing kisses comes to mind.

"It's my treat." She grins at the idea. "I want to thank the two people in my life who helped mold me into the person that I am."

"Aw." I run my hand over her dark curls. "I don't know whether to hug you or write an apology to your mother."

"Get over here." She pulls me in. Her boyfriend, Cole, gives a nod from behind as he hauls in more boxes. It's him I should write a thank you, too. He sort of got the ball rolling in the kisses department for me and Holt. A private smile creeps onto my lips because lately whenever

I think of Holt a silly grin wants to take up residency on my face.

Baya and Laney are here along with their respective fiancés, and we're quick to decorate the studio with crepe paper and the cardboard cutouts of ballet slippers I managed to excavate from the party supply store. Before I know it, throngs of bodies flood through the door along with my mother. Here she is with her signature fuchsia lipstick, her matching black Electric Lights Dance Studio T-shirt with the hot pink lettering. I watch as she works the room. Her smile never leaves her face. The entire first hour is peppered with her laughter, and it breaks my heart to think I might have knocked another deadbeat boyfriend out of her life. Not that he should have ever been in it to begin with.

"Hey"—I lean into Laney—"you should find someone for Mom." The two bozos she set me up with flash through my mind. "On second thought, maybe she's not so bad on her own."

"Are you kidding? She's a magnet for predators and felons."

I lock eyes with her a second. She said predator, and I wonder why she chose that word.

"You okay?" She bumps her hip into mine.

Holt walks in, and my entire person breathes a sigh of relief. My heart goes off like a bomb. My skin breaks out in a prickling heat. He smiles in my direction, and his grin lights up the entire room like a flash. Holt looks like a

Ralph Lauren model with his inky dark jeans, his button down baby blue shirt that makes his skin glow.

"Better than okay." My stomach bottoms out at the sight of him as I meet him halfway. "You're here." I wrap my arms around his waist and pull him in. It feels natural like this, and not a single part of me is concerned with the wandering eyes we might be attracting, namely my mother's.

"I'm not one to miss a good party." He brushes his cheek close to my neck and takes a deep breath. "Hope you don't mind, but once my brother mentioned he was headed over I didn't want to miss out. Besides, Annie needed a ride." He gives a sheepish smile.

"I wouldn't want it any other way," I say, fighting the urge to kiss him.

Laney comes over and frowns as Holt and I part ways.

"All right everybody." Mom claps her way to the center of the room. "First, I'd like to thank everybody here for coming out today and helping us celebrate twenty wonderful years at the ELDS." Wild applause breaks out. She glances around the studio brimming with old and new students. "As I look around at this room full of people, I can't help but think that each and every one of you contributed to the success of the Electric Lights Dance Studio. You built this place and all of the memories it stands on, literally step-by-step." Her eyes glitter with tears, and for the first time in my entire life I watch as a ball of liquid emotion rolls down her cheek.

Laney leans in. "*God*—she's human."

"I want you all to know that I love and appreciate each and every one of you," Mom continues through tears. "I couldn't have done any of this without you." She gives a hard sniff as another deafening applause breaks out. Her hands bat through the air until the noise dies down. "And, on that note, I'd like to invite up my daughter, my saving grace—Izzy, why don't you come here." She motions me over. I give a quick glance to Laney. I feel like crap when my mother treats me like an only child. "Izzy"—Mom comes over and pulls me in—"for the last several years you've been running this place like a pro, and I wracked my brain trying to think of how I can repay you. All I could come up with was this." She leans in and gives me a heartfelt hug.

Tears blur my vision as she holds on tight. I can't remember the last time my mother offered an embrace.

"I love you, mommy," I whisper just for her.

"I know," she whispers back.

I wipe down my face and call the lead dance team to the front. They step forward carefully unfurling a banner that reads *Thank you Ms. Bobbie for twenty fantastic years!* A colorful montage of signatures are scrawled out all over the sign—hundreds of sentiments from students old and new.

Tears roll down my mother's cheeks, in tandem, as she takes it all in.

My mother is a good person who deserves all of the good things life has to offer. I hope one day she finds someone deserving of her company, and, until that day happens, I'll make sure she always has me. I don't want her to ever be alone.

I look up, and Holt catches my eye.

I don't want to be alone either.

ജ്യോ

Once the studio clears out, Holt offers to help with the clean up. Laney and her friends took down most of the decorations before they left. Bryson took Annie home, so Holt and I have the studio to ourselves.

Holt dips his chin and looks at me from across the room like he's ready to pounce, and, holy hell, I'm not too sure I'd stop him if he tried. His eyes are on fire, and his smile is most definitely lewd. I'm liking the direction this is heading—a whole hell of a lot.

"Nice party, kitten." Holt strides over like a man on a mission.

"You know what I've always wanted to do?" I turn it to the last song on my phone and lock it in on a loop. Music filters through the air—a moody lyrical piece, rife with romantic implications.

"Test out the speakers when there's no one around?" He makes his way to me with his eyes glazed over, his lips already parting. Holt holds out a hand, and I take it.

"No, this." I wrap my arms around his waist, and he's quick to do the same. I've missed this with him since the moment we parted ways last week. I don't bother telling him this is my second slow dance with a man in my entire life and that he's that man.

"You're pretty good at this." He dips his face into my neck and unabashedly takes a deep breath.

"Why are you always sniffing me?" I hold back the giggle ricocheting in my chest.

"Why do you always smell so damn good?" He lands a cushioned kiss over my neck, and I pull back. "Sorry." He blinks a quick smile.

"Don't be. In fact, put your lips back there." I take a deep breath and feel his body crushing over mine. "I was enjoying that."

Holt complies without a word, and his mouth lands over my neck in a series of butter soft kisses trailing up to my ear.

"Are you feeling this?" he whispers.

"God, yes—it feels amazing."

"I mean us." He tucks the words hot in my ear.

I freeze for a moment before forcing my muscles to move in time with his. There. I've done it. I've toyed with his emotions, and now I've landed us in this questionable place.

"Holt"—I pull back—"I can't date you."

"Why not?" His Adam's apple rises and falls as if a tragedy were about to unfold, and I think it is.

"Because." I shrug, trying to lighten the mood. "I'd have to dye my hair blonde and outfit my wardrobe with skanky clothes. Which I may or may not already own." I bite over my lip as if I were trying to shake up his Levis. "Plus, I'd have to dust off my bombshell bra, and that thing really cuts into my back." I shake my head as if this were a real issue, and, even though it is, I don't think I've managed to add any levity to the situation. Holt wants something more, and I think I do, too.

My mother's banner catches my eye. The night of my eighteenth birthday flashes through my mind, unexpected as a grease fire. I can hear his taunting voice. Feel his hands pressing in, snaking all over my body and no matter how hard I try to shake the image out of my head, it won't leave me alone.

"I'm sorry. I have to go." I pull back. "You have to go." I rake my fingers through my hair. "I have to lock up." I bolt for my phone and pluck the wire from it, filling the room with a deafening silence.

"Whoa—I'm sorry." He takes a step toward me, and I back away without meaning to. "Izzy." His eyes fill with heartbreak as he takes me in.

"It's not you. It's me, Holt. I'm damaged—nothing or no one can ever fix that. You deserve someone whole and happy." Tears come uninvited, and I'm unable to blink them away. "You deserve someone who'll make you happy."

"*You* make me happy, Iz." He holds out his hand. His lips fill in a deep shade of crimson. His face turns ashen. "Let me do this with you. We can get help. We can find someone you can talk to." He pleads with tears of his own brimming to the surface.

"Please, just get out." I spin around.

"Iz, you can't mean that." He places his hand on my shoulder, and I prove unmovable. "We can push through this. I want to help you. Let me be there for you."

I don't say a word. Holt drips his hand down my back, slow, hot as lava, and eventually his footsteps drift toward the exit.

"I'm still here for you, Iz."

I wait until I can't hear his footsteps anymore. The sound of an engine roaring to life fills the silence, and I fall to the floor in a heap of tears.

This time they're not for my mother.

This time they're all for me.

Holt

A week bleeds by and no sign of Izzy at the bar. I've tried calling her twice, but she won't pick up, and there's only so much rejection my ego can take. So I do the next best thing, I ply her closest friend with free drinks until she sings like a bird.

A group of coeds walk through the door just as I'm pouring the third beer down Jemma Jackson's throat. So far I've learned there's far too much drama and trauma in this woman's life for me to ever keep track of and, also, she might be on the lookout for husband number four.

"So what's going on with Izzy these days?" I try to sound cool about it as if we were just shooting the breeze.

She lets out a loud whoop of a laugh, and Laney looks over from the bar.

Shit. I hadn't noticed she walked in, and I know for a fact she's not on the schedule tonight. Laney breezes over without missing a beat.

"What's up?" She pulls up a seat, stern as shit. She's knows I'm up to no good, I can tell by that disapproving smirk on her face. It's the same look Izzy gave me last week just before she told me to get the hell out of her life—give or take a few sentiments.

"We were just about to discuss your sister," Jemma slurs before letting out a belch that has me sliding my seat back a good two feet.

"Holy crap, Edwards." Laney slaps her hands down over Jemma's keys and sinks them into her pocket.

"There was no way in hell I was going to let her take off." God's honest truth. When Baya came along, we implemented the "sorry Charlie" program, and we've never looked back. Not one drunk ass is allowed to get up and drive.

"And what's this we're discussing about my sister?" Laney pulls a forced grin across her face because we both know she's putting my balls on notice. "I hear she's well. And you, Holt, have you heard from her lately?"

Here we go. "No, I haven't." It's like stepping on a landmine. I know better than to piss Laney off.

"Really? Okay, so it looks like the math is pretty simple. Izzy plus no contact with Holt equals she's not interested." Laney doesn't hesitate with the sting.

"Oh, she's interested." Jemma gives a circular nod. "She's so puma." She rakes her hand through the air like she's about to claw my head off. "*Rawr!*" She screeches so loud half the bar turns around. "No, not puma, she's so—cougar!" She shouts as if guessing an answer on a game show. "She's *the cougar*." Her eyes close as she rolls her head over her neck. "Izzy—cougar—*rawr*."

"Oh, hon," Laney moans. "Holt and I will get you some coffee." She pulls me up by the ear until we're clear across the room.

"Ouch." I gently remove Laney's pincer grasp from my earlobe. "What was that for?"

"What was that for?" She points hard at the pile of blonde hair that's currently lying over the table.

"She was thirsty." I give a slight scowl at the puddle of a woman I've turned Jemma into. "And I'm pretty damn thirsty, too." I take a step toward Laney. She looks so much like Izzy it hurts. "What's going on with your sister? She's all messed up, Laney." My voice cracks. "I want to help her, and she won't let me."

"What are you talking about?" She takes a step back as if I were out of my mind, and I wish I were. "There's nothing wrong with my sister."

"Something or someone tore her apart. She's injured on the inside, and that's about as far as she let me in."

"Oh my, God." Laney clasps her hand around her throat while looking over at Jemma. "There is something, then." She swallows hard. "I think Jemma knows." She shakes her head before burying her face in her hands. "God, I'm such a lousy sister. I have no clue what it could be." She looks up at me with those serious navy eyes, and all I see is Izzy. "I'll try to get her to open up. She's got another blind date this Thursday. What better day than the Fourth to make the sparks fly—right?" She gives a little shrug. "Anyway, I thought we were close. I thought I knew all of Izzy's secrets, and now I feel like nothing more than a stranger. Isn't that something? The person you thought you knew best, you don't know at all." She takes off toward the kitchen in a daze.

Funny, I've felt that way for years, only in my family it's me that nobody really knows. I'm the charred branch of the family tree, the invisible stain that no one quite realizes. And, if I get my way, it's going to stay like that forever.

No use in making a bad situation worse.

But if it's such a good idea to keep my mouth shut why the hell do I feel so bad about it?

Izzy flashes through my mind. She'll be here in two days.

Maybe it's not so important that I know what's killing her on the inside—at least not yet.

Maybe all she needs is for someone to give her space—to love her on her own terms. And that's exactly what I plan on doing.

That is if she gives me another chance.

And I'm hoping she will.

ജ‍ഇ

Wednesday night after a long line of shit bands perform, if you can call it that, Bryson sits both Cole and me down.

"What's up?" I ask, landing between them.

"Just thinking about what Dad said a few weeks back. I'm not sure I'm ready to part with this place."

Dad owns more than the Black Bear, there's the Ice Bar, and Sky Lab. I try to make an appearance at the other locations at least twice a month, but with Izzy on my brain, I haven't done that lately.

"I've been thinking about it, too." Damn straight I have. This is it for me. I don't have a fancy degree to hang on my wall or flaunt in any prospective employer's face for that matter. This is do or die for me, and to hell if my father thinks I'm going down with this place. "I'm going to buy him out."

"Are you serious?" Cole deadpans. "Dude, you work for tips. How the hell are you going to bankroll three different bars?"

"It's called a loan, moron. If I don't qualify, I'll see if I can get my mother to cosign. I'll sell that damn boat I never see anymore. Every little bit helps, right? I'll do what I have to." I've thought it through enough to have worked out any impending details. Lost about a week's worth of sleep over the idea, too.

"You're just going to pick up and run this place, huh?" Bryson smacks his lips together as if I'd have better luck laying a golden egg.

"Yes—exactly the way I have been."

"You don't have any clue how to pay the bills. Mom has a small army working the back office—and payroll? You have any idea about that?"

"I'm a quick learner."

"Really? And how do you know this?" Bryson crosses his arms as if he were amused. "You haven't set foot in a classroom in the last five years."

"All right." I stand up with my arms in the air. Swear to God, if he were closer, I'd deck him. "I get it. I'm too freaking stupid in your eyes because I don't have a four-year degree to shove down everyone's throat for the rest of my life. Well, have a great rest of yours because if you're going to be throwing that shit in my face every chance you get, feel free to stay the fuck away from me." I kick my chair back as I leave.

I wondered if it was coming. Bryson has never been an ass about our educational differences, but now that he's got that hot little degree in his hands, he's settling into becoming a self-righteous prick.

I take off into the cool night, hop in my truck and just drive.

Sure wish Izzy was here filling that seat beside me.

But then nothing ever seems to go my way.

It probably shouldn't.

Great Sexpectations

Izzy

Dear Dad,

It's safe to say I've fucked up my fair share of things in life (excuse the language). Usually it's things I don't intend on ruining that sort of unravel because of me— such as Mom and her revolving door boyfriends. But this time I've delved into new territory. I've managed to screw up something sweet that might have led to interesting places—hell, good places. Anyway, I've finally become a master at sabotaging my own life. Just because something pretty terrible happened to me once doesn't mean I should let it terrorize me for the rest of my days. But then that's logic and my mind seems to run on anything but. Plus there's Mom. You may have left her, but I'm the reason she's truly alone. Sure wish she'd meet someone halfway decent. I'd take a quarter decent at this point.

~See ya.

Fucking up in Hollow Brook (Happy now? Without you my language is in the shitter. I hope you feel a little guilty. You should.)

~Iz

 howzbegin

By the time my cats finish their tap dance routine on my back, Mom already has the coffee brewing. I used to enjoy a good cat stomping, but their light-footed paws don't even come close to Holt's magic fingers. A wave of grief washes over me. As cruel as I was to him the other day, I think we both know it's for the best. Holt deserves someone capable of navigating her way through the day without choking on the smoke from a fire that burned out a long time ago. That's all I ever seem to do these days, gag on the memories that have wrapped themselves around my neck like a noose.

"Well, it's official"—Mom slams the fridge shut with a package of bacon fisted in her hand—"Don says he's not coming back. Wouldn't say why." She huffs her way over to the stove and starts up the flame so fast it almost singes her brows. "Damn men. Never know a good thing when they see it." She opens and slams the cabinets until she finds the pan she's looking for while continuing her rant about *damn men*. She's used that phrase so often over the course of my life, I'm almost positive that's the proper way to address them.

"I'm telling you, Iz"—she huffs it out—"finding an upstanding man who would die for you—who would *kill* for you..." She loses herself in a daze just staring at that half empty bottle of my father's whiskey. "It's like finding a pot of gold. You find one like that—you know you've struck it rich. Sometimes I think love is the only fortune that matters."

Holt runs through my mind with his high-voltage smile, his bedroom eyes that have already had me twelve different ways. Holt said he wanted to help. He wanted to push through this thing, whatever it was, together. Heck, I don't even know what it is. All I know is that my mind fractured like a mirror one day, and here I am almost ten years later still cutting myself on the shards.

"So I've been thinking." She heads back to the fridge and pulls out a carton of eggs. "I haven't really been spending time at the studio, and you've more than picked up the slack."

"Sounds like you've got your head screwed on straight." For once. "You've been thinking right." I pluck a banana off the counter and pour myself a cup of coffee. Mom has been persona non grata as of late, but, now that her ankle is better, I'm sure she'll be back full steam ahead.

"I don't know if I told you, but I've had three different investors contact me about the studio." Her eyes narrow in on mine, with their blue topaz prisms. My mother was voted Ms. All American her senior year in high school. She was a stunner, and, if you could look past all the rage that boils in her these days, she still is.

"Investors, huh? Sounds like we should consider stock options." A surge of adrenaline rockets through me. "I've always felt the studio should franchise. Do you know we have over fifteen families that have moved to Hollow Brook just so their daughters could participate at Electric Lights? Half the time, I'm wondering if we know what we've got. I have all kinds of ideas that could help streamline the business from teaching techniques, right down to office work. With a little elbow grease, I think I can get the studio in top running condition before Laney ever says I do."

"That's not what I'm talking about." She turns the burners down and takes a seat across from me at the table. "Izzy." She folds her hands and looks into my eyes as if she's about to dispense life changing news. God, maybe she's ready to pass the baton and give me the business? I've wanted that—hoped for it. Heck, I think I expected it on some level. "The reason I've had so many investors look into the dance studio is because I'm in talks with a real estate agent."

"Real estate? Are you thinking about selling the house?" My hair stands on end at the thought. When my father left, my mother whisked us away to a faraway town where no one knew our shame. We came with nothing and no one to call our own except this tiny piece of real estate my mother purchased. And now this was our house. Our dingy yellow walls, our weed-riddled yard. This was more than our home. It took the place of my father when he left us all those years ago. It's strong and loyal and managed to stay in one place unlike the man that ran out on us.

"Izzy." She lets out a breath, slow and full of frustration. The bacon starts to burn, but she doesn't pay it any attention. "It's the *studio* I'm looking to sell."

"What?" I bounce back in my seat, holding onto the lip of the table as if it were anchoring me from drifting away. I was wrong. It wasn't just the house that held us together after my father left—it was the studio. They're my brick and mortar parents that I love as much as the real deals. And why I still love my father after what he did is a mystery to me.

"This is exactly why I wasn't looking forward to telling you." She says it sweetly, and, ironically, in a maternal tone I've never heard before. "I've given that studio everything I've got. I think it's holding me back. If I hadn't been married to that damn box all those years I might have a normal life right now, and, truthfully, it kills me to see you going down the same path."

"Oh, please." I jump to my feet trying to hold back a laugh. "So now you're pissed at the studio because of your poor choice in men? How about having some standards? How about meeting someone and scoping out their morals before you let them shack up with you, and your two young daughters!" My voice rises to the ceiling before ricocheting off all four walls. "How about you open your *damn eyes* and see that the fallout of your actions cost me so much more than I was ever willing to give!" I knock the chair over, grab my purse, and get the hell out.

I don't know if I'll ever come back.

I'm so damn sick of protecting everyone all the time.

And, as usual, it's me I forgot to protect.

⁞⁞

The Fourth of July is next to Valentine's Day as far as couples holidays go. I found out the hard way one year when Laney invited me out with her friends, and it turned into one big make-out session with me being the only one focusing on the explosives in the sky. Nevertheless it's the Fourth, and, oddly enough, tonight is the third blind disaster Laney has set up for me. Three strikes and she's out. Those are the rules, and I'm sticking to them.

I'm not sure what has Laney so motivated to boot me over to testosterone-laden pastures other than the fact she may not like having her sister turn into an old maid right before her eyes. Too bad. Not only have I been an old maid in training since my eighteenth birthday, but I'm driving the bandwagon for future old maids of America. I might even start an alliance. Of course, there will be a four-cat minimum for admittance into the organization. Bonus points if you live with your mother. A spot on the board if she happens to be a battle-ax that prefers pond scum sleeping next to her at night.

All the way over to the Black Bear, the conversation, or more like shouting match, I had with my mother replays on a loop.

"Sell the studio," I whisper, shaking my head as I enter the bar. My mother is out of her fuchsia-lipped, headband-wearing mind. First she wanted to fire up the RV with Don, and now she's trying to sell the studio? It's obvious she's having a midlife crisis. That studio takes better care of us than any man ever could. It puts food on the table, keeps a roof over our heads, and has turned every girl that's ever graced those halls into an extended family member—not to mention a seasoned dancer.

Inside, the Black Bear is thick with people. The heavy scent of fajitas permeates the air, and, sure enough, I catch Laney carrying a sizzling platter to a nearby table. I do a quick scan of the bar and spot Bryson and Cole. Down at the far end, ensconced with a pair of amply endowed girls that look far younger than Laney, is Holt.

My heart sinks at the sight. A jealous fire rages through my bones, and a part of me says that's my Holt. But he's not. At least he shouldn't be.

I step into the crowd and bump into a body—Baya.

"Hey!" She jumps as if she's genuinely happy to see me. "Rumor has it you have a hot date in T-minus five minutes. Your sister is freaking out. For some reason she was afraid you wouldn't show."

"I'm here. Ready for dating duty."

She clicks her tongue at me. "It's not a chore, Izzy. I promise tonight's offering is a drool worthy specimen who has his head on straight."

"We'll see." For as little as Laney has been screening the prospects, I'm sure Baya knows them that much less.

"No, really. He works for Ryder's father. He's got his MBA and everything."

MBA? A wave of heat floods through me. I wonder how Laney sold me? I have the furthest thing from an MBA. Hell, I barely got out of high school with a C average.

"Nice. Tell Laney I'll be back in the corner." I wanted to say *nobody puts Izzy in a corner*—with the exception of Laney. But Baya is so young she probably wouldn't get the reference. We part ways, and I take the long way to the back in an effort to avoid walking past the bar. I stride by a halfway decent looking guy sitting alone, perusing the menu, and he holds up a finger as I'm about to pass him.

"Izzy Sawyer?" His pale green eyes connect with mine as he gives a pleasant smile. He's about my age with deep-welled dimples and dark, thick hair, eyes that command my attention. He's abnormally handsome, but something deep inside me is already holding him at bay.

"That would be me."

He's quick to stand. "You're even more beautiful than your sister let on. Wyatt James." He offers his hand, and I take it, strong yet gentle as he gives a solid shake.

"I'm impressed. You're early." I take a seat across from him. My eyes skirt the bar to see if Holt is still sandwiched between the cleavage-wielding cheer squad, and, to my horror there are at least four more girls surrounding him, creating a bubble of silicone. Should we have an earthquake, Holt is well protected.

Crap. At least I know that cutting all ties with him was the right thing to do. God knows I'd hate to slow down his mojo. I frown because I hate the thought of his mojo being spread out over all of Hollow Brook without me.

"I like being punctual," he says, trying to pull me back into the moment. "I'm not one to keep a pretty girl waiting. You hungry?"

"You're not going to ask me to run my feet through a spongy dessert are you?" I pick up the menu and glance over it. I think I have it memorized by now.

"I wasn't—but it sounds like a neat trick."

He leans in, and his warm cologne washes over me. It's a touch more vibrant than the one Holt wears. More spice than I'm comfortable with, and it makes me miss Holt that much more.

Wyatt looks decent, and, for the most part, sane, but, in truth, I'm growing impatient just sitting around waiting for his insanity to sprout from his head like horns.

I put down the menu, and he does the same.

"Okay, give it to me." I fold my arms and wait for it. "You like mountain climbing at midnight? Running up fire escapes more your thing? Let me guess—you have an entire closet full of women's clothes you're just dying to show off. Maybe a little lingerie runway action?"

The smile glides off his face. He dips his chin and examines me as if I've just confessed to killing his puppy, and now I feel like a bag of crap that just accidentally set itself on fire.

"Fire escapes?" He shakes his head. "Not my thing. I am into spontenatiy though. How about we blow this place and catch the next flight to Europe? I've got a backpack I've been meaning to dust off and a few McDonald's gift certificates I'm looking to blow. We can eat cheeseburgers while walking down the Champs-Elysees." He leans in serious as death. "How would you like to wolf down a pack of French fries at the Eifel Tower?"

Holy hell. Knew it. He's as psychotic as they come with his handsome face, that quasi-arrogant air about him, and all he wants to do is have a carb fest in the city of lights.

"And"—he folds his hands and bounces them on the table—"since we're getting close, I'd like the passwords to your phone and email accounts. Honesty is the best policy, and there's nowhere better to start than the beginning. Of course, I'll let you glance at mine if you want, but you can take my word for it. I'm as trustworthy as they come." His lips pull back in a manufactured smile, and I've either just been bested, or Laney has topped herself with this one.

"Are you for real?"

"I am for real." His shoulders relax. "But it sounds like you've had your fair share of fun-filled blind dates, and I didn't want to go down as vanilla." He slumps in his seat. "How'd I do?"

"I almost bolted at 'passwords.'" I strum my fingers over the table to keep from laughing. "You were anything but vanilla."

Laney comes by, and we put in an order for shrimp fajitas and a couple of non-alcoholic beers. We talk for what feels like hours about life, Hollow Brook, the bands we listened to in high school—which happen to be the exact same ones. Then it hits me. Not every man out there is a loon. Not every man out there is in on some conspiracy to control women, to steal forty-five dollars out of their wallets, or to mistreat them in some misogynistic way. Wyatt James is an overall nice guy. He'll be a great catch for someone, someday.

I cut a quick glance to the bar where my eyes have wandered all night. Holt stands alone, wiping down a martini glass, looking as if someone just handed him his balls on a shrimp fajita platter. I can't help feeling like that someone was me.

"So you almost ready to move this party to the beach and check out the fireworks?" Wyatt asks as kind as possible, and not a single part of me is revolted or afraid he's planning to kidnap me before the grand finale.

"I think I am." I bite down on a nervous smile because I've never done what I'm about to do next. "But I think this is where we should part ways. I think you're a really nice guy. And I believe with all my heart there's a really nice girl out there for you. It's just—she's not me."

"Really?" He looks puzzled, but the smile still lingers on his lips. "I thought we were getting along great. But I get it. If you're not feeling it, I appreciate you putting me out of my misery sooner than later. If you ever need anything, you know where to find me." He offers his hand, and I shake it. "It was real nice meeting you, Izzy Sawyer. Take care. You deserve someone nice yourself."

We stand, and I watch as he takes off into the crowd. A breath of relief streams through my lungs.

It would have been easy to keep talking with Wyatt, to go the beach and watch the fireworks, maybe set off a few of our own—to keep him in my life in general.

I turn toward the bar, and Holt catches my eye.

But there's already a man who's stolen my heart, and I think it's time I let him know how I feel.

I head over to him with my eyes locked over his. Holt freezes with his dishtowel still stuck in a glass. The electric blue lights that trim the bar illuminate him like an angel ready to avenge.

"How did it go?" Holt buries a smile deep in his cheek, and my insides erupt in flames.

"It came and went."

"So what was his thing? Did he offer to cast a mold of your feet and build a shrine? Find the highest rooftop and repel down using your hair?"

A laugh trembles from me, and, for the first time in a good long while, I feel relaxed, at home. Holt always makes me feel at home.

"He didn't have a thing. He was smart, thoughtful, kind, and he has an alarmingly normal sense of humor."

Holt plunks his glass on the counter. His chest pumps as he takes a deep breath.

"So—you think he's the one?"

I step in with my knees shaking, my throat dry, gritty as sandpaper.

"No, I think you are."

Holt

All those years ago, when I first laid eyes on Izzy, all I could think about was how beautiful she was. Here we are, almost a decade later, and she hasn't changed a bit. Only now, I would stake my life on the fact I just misheard her.

"You think *I'm* the one?" I tilt my ear in her direction in the event she plans on clearing the air right here and now.

"Yes." She softens toward me. "I'm not interested in anybody else, Holt. I'm interested in you. You're my pot of gold, and I don't want to let you go."

Pot of gold? I can roll with that. A grin breaks loose on my face.

"You want to head to the beach and watch the fireworks? I've got a boat we can take out if you want." It takes everything in me not to hop the bar and scoop her up in my arms.

A smile inches up her face. Her lashes lower seductively. "I was sort of hoping we could see them from your place."

"Done." Hot damn. "Cole." I nod over at him as I make my way around the bar. "Man the fort would you?" It's pretty much dead right now. The closer it gets to sundown, the fewer people we'll have. Everyone is out enjoying the evening, sipping cold ones while sitting next to a fire, so I don't feel too bad about taking off early.

"I got this." He nods over to Iz with approval. "Have fun."

"Already am," I whisper.

Izzy wraps her arms around my waist, and we walk out of the bar like that—like a real couple.

A wave of sweet summer air hits us as we head into the parking lot. I walk her over to her Civic which happens to be parked right next to my truck, and I take it as an omen of good things to come.

Izzy pulls me in tight.

"So"—I land a kiss over her forehead, and my muscles relax for the first time in a week—"what makes you so sure I'm the one?"

"You make me feel safe, Holt." She shakes her head. "Do you think I might be the one for you?"

"I know it." I lean in and cover her mouth with mine. Our tongues mingle in a bout of foreplay like I've never experienced before, slow and measured as if to prove the point we have all of time to do just this.

I never thought I deserved something this good—still don't.

But I'm no fool, there's no way in hell I'm letting Izzy go.

ଛୠ

"Whiskey sour?" Izzy offers a restrained smile as I pass her the drink and drop down next to her on the bench swing. I've got a pretty decent view of the Hollow Brook skyline from the balcony, and there's usually a fireworks show at the park down the street, so I'm betting we'll have front row seats.

"I cut it with a little Sprite." I hold up my own glass. "Bottoms up?"

"I think I'll nurse mine."

I pull her over to me, and we sit and watch the night sky as the sound of fireworks go off in the distance every now and again.

Izzy spins into me with her drink cradled against my chest. "So how are we going to do this?" She whispers out of breath as if she were anxious for the answer. And I wish I had one to give her.

"I think we're doing it. One day at a time."

"Baby steps," we say in unison.

"Jinx." I lean down and steal a kiss off her lips.

Izzy moans with approval and tugs at my lips with hers. She pulls back and touches the whisky to her mouth. "It's good. I approve."

"I'm glad."

"You'll never guess what bomb my mother decided to drop on me this morning."

"I'm not the explosive in question am I? Let the record show I've always had a healthy fear of Bobbie Sawyer."

She gives a little laugh, and her hair spills over my chest like a dark scarf.

"No, it has everything to do with the studio. She wants to sell it." Her features melt with grief. I know for a fact that studio is like a second home to Izzy, sort of the way the bar is mine.

"Sounds like we have a lot more in common than we thought." I tell her all about the talk my father had a few weeks back. "I think I'm going to take the place over myself. I just need to figure out a way to buy out my parents." I pinch my eyes shut a moment. "It's going to be a bitch, but I know I can do it."

"Holt." She pulls back with a laugh caught in her throat. "I think that's fantastic. Do you think I'd be able to pull off something like that?"

"I don't see why not. Heck, maybe your mother would go easy on you and let you take over payments. With my father remarrying a gold digger, who wants to turn those vodka bottles into shoes, it's a little more complicated. But I know you, Iz, you've been running that place on your own since as far back as I can remember. You've got this. Are you sure it's something you want?"

"Want?" She shakes her head and takes another sip. "It's something I *need*. I can't imagine my future without the studio in it. It's been the anchor in my life for as long as I can remember. That's my baby." She settles those blazing eyes over me and brushes her fingers across the stubble on my cheeks. "You're perfect, you know that?"

Izzy stills. Her breathing all but stops. "What do you think people will say about us?"

"Who the hell cares what they say. But, if I had to guess, I'm betting they'll say we're damn lucky. That's all anyone should ever say about us." I sink a kiss over her lips again, and her tongue meets up with mine. The fireworks start up, and we miss the first ten minutes.

Izzy rests her head on my chest as we catch the grand finale. So many brilliant sparks lighting up the night and then they're gone in seconds, nothing but a memory. I can't help but wonder if that's what will happen to us. I started a chain of heartbreak years ago, and I've always thought it should end with me. But I'll fight to keep that from happening to the two of us. She's the first and only girl I'd fight all of hell to keep safe from the curse I've brought on my family.

"What are you thinking?" Her voice rises, soft as smoke.

"I'd fight for you, Izzy. We're right and nobody can tell us otherwise."

She looks up as her eyes shine into mine.

"I don't think we should finish the whiskey, Holt."

"Why's that?" A smile tugs on my lips, but I won't give it.

"Because I want us to be sober for what happens next. I've waited far too long for this moment, and I want to remember it. I want you to remember it. I want us to be present with body, heart, and soul for the things we're about to share."

My balls pulsate like a bomb.

"And what things are those?" My lids grow heavy with lust. It's taking all of my strength not to pin her to the floor and make love to her right here under the stars both real and manufactured.

"The thing I'm glad I saved most—me." She picks up the whiskey sour. "One last sip—a gift from me to you." She takes a final hit before setting the glass down. Her lips find mine, and I pull the liquor right out of her mouth. Her hands wander up my shirt as the taste of whiskey permeates our kisses. I'll never be able to look at a bottle again without thinking of Izzy.

"That was one hell of a show," she whispers, tracking kisses all the way to my ear. "You think you can top that?"

A gentle laugh rolls through me. "Oh, sweetie, I know I can."

I dig my fingers into her hips as our mouths get lost in one another again.

"How about we take this party somewhere private?" Her lips quiver a bright ruby red. Izzy is glassy-eyed and hopped up on anything but liquor.

"You sure you want to do this?"

"You're the one who promised to teach me everything and anything I ever wanted to know." She lowers her lids just enough. "I want to know the things you do, Holt. I'm ready to go there if you are."

If I had any question on whether or not Izzy was a virgin, I think it's just been answered. How the hell that happened I have no clue, but I'm damn glad about it. I'd be a liar if I didn't say I was dying for this moment for as long as I can remember, and now it's that much sweeter.

She presses her lips to my chin. "You in?"

"All the way, baby."

"Good." Her eyes widen as if she were surprised after all. "You'll be my first, Holt." Her cheeks redden a deep shade of burgundy, and, in this dim light, Izzy becomes her own shadow.

"I'm glad." I dot her lips with a simple kiss. "I'm hoping to be your last."

I scoop her into my arms as we make our way inside. Izzy pulls me down by the neck, and our lips fuse over one another as if we were putting out a fire in each other's mouths. I kick the screen shut with my foot, but I couldn't care less if an entire swarm of mosquitoes flew in. There's not a single thing that could spoil this night.

"You sure about this?" I whisper straight into her mouth through a kiss.

"Positive." She rakes her fingernails over my bare chest until it feels as if she's about to draw blood. But I don't mind. I want it to hurt, to feel good, to do both at the very same time.

We engage in one long lip-lock, bumping down the hall as I carry her to the bedroom. I send up a quick prayer, hoping it doesn't smell like a pile of old gym socks. But I don't notice the smell or the fact that I've got stacks of crap lying around waiting to greet her in the morning. None of it matters. Right now this is about us, Izzy and

Holt, two names I'm hoping will one day be synonymous with one another.

My father and that fucked-up summer bounces through my mind. I don't think I can live with that guilt forever. Maybe sometime soon I'll try to figure a way out of that hell. I think I've suffered enough. I think we all have.

I sit Izzy down on the edge of the bed and slowly take off my T-shirt. There's just enough moonlight streaming in, highlighting us until we look like a pair of apparitions. I run my fingers through her hair, soft and slick like strands of silk that go on forever.

Izzy dips her fingers into the lip of my jeans and plays with the button until it gives. She lowers the zipper without ever taking her eyes off mine and gives my boxers a firm tug. I reach down and pull off her top in one easy move. Izzy's skin glows like marble. The shadow of her bra hugs her curves in all the right places. I reach back and unhook it, holding it together a moment as I lock eyes with hers. She gives a knowing smile as if to say she's still on board, and that's all the reassurance I need.

Izzy slinks out of her bra and tosses it in the corner. She falls back on her elbows, exposing herself with her perfect tits splayed out just for me.

"*Fuck*," I whisper.

Izzy blows out a breath as she tugs down my Levis, and my boxers flee right along with them.

This is it, the point of no return, and I'm damn glad about it.

I steady my knees to either side of her as I dive in for a kiss. My dick scrapes against her bare stomach, and she cinches with a laugh.

"Hello," she says, wrapping her fingers around it. "Nice to meet you, too."

"He's dying to get to know you better."

"Maybe he should come inside and stay a while?" She teases, pulling me over her in the process.

I reach down and work like hell to get those skintight jeans off her body. She slinks right out of them and they thump to the floor with a pronounced finality.

This is it—nothing but skin over skin. The moment I've spent half my life dreaming of is actually here with the girl I've always loved. A part of me wants to say those words. To say them every minute of every day until it sinks in for her. If anyone deserves to be loved it's Izzy. But I don't plan on spooking her—baby steps. For now I'll just have to show her how I feel. Make love to every inch of her, and that's exactly what I plan on doing all night long.

I reach to the nightstand and pull out a condom, hold it up to the light for her to inspect.

She gives a little laugh. "Is this the part where I say trick or treat?"

"You don't have to. I plan on delivering both."

Her chest rumbles with a laugh and takes me with it. "That's exactly what I was hoping you'd say."

"If you're nice, I might throw in a few fireworks." I run my lips in long, hot tracks all the way down her neck. "Aw, hell—for you, kitten? I'll throw a few in anyway."

She arches her back, pressing her tits in my chest, and I die a little on the inside.

Izzy pulls me in and takes a gentle bite out of my ear.

"I feel like I'm going to bring down the party with my lack of carnal knowledge," she whispers it low like a secret.

"Don't count on it. But I think it's too much to teach in just one session," I tease. "We'll have to make this a reoccurring event."

"Oh, is that right?" She rakes her nails over my back, soft as a feather. "You up for nightly sessions?"

I look down at Izzy with the smile dissipating from my lips because things just got serious, and I want to remember everything about this moment.

"I have nothing against the morning or afternoon either," I whisper.

"Lucky for me, I've got nowhere to go tomorrow."

"That's funny, I was just about to write myself off the schedule."

"Sounds like a great idea." She digs her fingers into my hair.

I wash my eyes over her, naked in my bed with her knees cradling either side of my chest, and I still can't believe it.

"We're a great idea." My mouth lands over hers, exploding with every emotion I've ever felt for her.

This is happening.

We're happening.

And for the first time in a long while, I don't feel an ounce of guilt over how happy I am.

I hope it lasts.

I hope Izzy and I last, too.

The Beginning of Us

Izzy

Dear Dad,

Sometimes life has a way of surprising you, in a good way. I'm okay with that. More than okay.

Almost happy for once,
~Iz

If I could describe my life in colors it would begin with a pure azure blue the exact color of my father's eyes, then, after he left, an entire sea of navy to represent the long dark night he cast us into. The black of midnight would come in right at my eighteenth birthday. It created a stain that bled through for almost ten long years. Then this new world Holt has brought me into, first yellow, then orange, then red with aching passion. We were ripping through every shade of pink, electric blue, green as bright as springtime, peaches and creams, the deep salmon of a brand new day. Every color was present and accounted for. They were all here, in every hue, with Holt spilling them at my feet like a deck of playing cards. We had unearthed one of life's biggest secrets, how to push past the darkness and fall madly, deeply in ruby red love. And, although I'm not ready to say those words—to hear them—I'm ready to live them, to let them vibrate over me in a rainbow poured out from the hot of Holt's mouth, from the weight of his steely body over mine. Holt is delivering me from the darkness, taking me by the hand and leading me out of those charred woods I lost myself in so long ago. I don't know how to thank him. I don't think there are enough thank yous to let him know how indebted to him I really am. Holt is the only man I've ever felt comfortable with. The only one that doesn't make me feel as if I want to jump out of my own skin simply from being in the same vicinity. Holt makes me feel at ease. He makes me *crave* his kisses, addictive as candy. And now I want all of him, covering me, in me—buried deep inside where he can never come out.

I run my hands down the hard ridges of his abs, lower still until my fingers run through the curls at the base of his hips, and I'm holding him—*holding* him right there in my hands. My fingers run up and down, taking in the slight curve, feeling the ridges, and, for a fleeting moment, I want to tell him there's no way in hell this is ever going to fit inside me.

"You okay?" He presses a warm kiss onto my forehead, and the shadow of a smile etches up his cheek.

"Better than okay. You sure this is all right?" I give him a slight squeeze, and Holt trembles with a quiet laugh. "I mean if you've been harboring a *big*, bad secret, now would be a good time to tell me."

"I promise it was made just for you. It'll be perfect." He dots another sweet kiss to my lips and falls back on the bed, tearing open the condom wrapper and pulling out the shadowed disc. "It's sticky—you probably don't want to touch it."

"Sticky, huh?" I run my finger over it to affirm this.

Here I am, thrust in a brand new world—one that my friends, my sister, entered into forever ago. My heart pounds as if it's trying to hammer its way out. My body goes numb as the gravity of what's about to happen sinks in.

"I must be laughable to you."

"What?" He rolls it on, and I defiantly run my finger down his rock hard curve one more time. Still sticky. "Izzy." Holt leans in until his warm breath brushes over my cheek. "I don't know what happened that left you so hurt, but I promise—you're everything good in my life. I will always be here for you. We fit—deep down inside, we're the same person. I've wanted you as a part of my life ever since I stepped in that dance studio when I was just a kid. It was you, Izzy. Every day since that moment it's only been you my heart has wanted."

My breathing picks up as my mind swirls with thoughts of that fated day. Is it a coincidence that Holt was there that afternoon, venerating my beauty through his starry eyes, and that it's him who's pulling me through to the other side of this great ache that swallowed me whole so long ago?

"I remember that day." I dig my head into the pillow. "And now I want to build new memories."

"I'm in." Holt gently cradles the back of my neck, pulling me closer until a breath can't be squeezed between us.

His mouth crashes over mine. Holt sings my praises, venerates my beauty once again by way of his white-hot, electric kisses. These were impassioned pleas for me to hear him, to feel his affection, and I want to. I want it all with Holt.

I pull him down and feel his weight as he lays his chest to mine.

"Izzy"—he draws back until our eyes connect, and my adrenaline rockets through my skull—"I'm in love—"

I touch my finger to his lips and shake my head ever so slightly.

"No words," I whisper as tears blur my vision. I can't go there. I'm not ready. Don't know if I'll ever be.

I pull my knees up and guide him in, closing my eyes, just feeling the burn as Holt becomes a part of me in the most intimate way.

He lets out a groan—a roar—as if he's had it pent up all along. I arch my head into the pillow and bite down hard over my lip. Holt presses in, pushing deeper as my body fights him every inch of the way. He leans down and peppers my face with heated kisses before pulling out and starting in on a slow and easy rhythm. My body starts to give. My legs relax over his back as he thrusts in and out with far more ease. Every last part of me surrenders to him, and I open up for Holt like a moonflower. Here it is—done, in the record books. Holt Edwards is my first, and, lucky for me, he wants to be my last.

Holt reaches down and threads his fingers through mine. He pulls my hands over my head as he continues to move his body in mine. This feels right, natural, and pure. Not one part of me wants to run screaming. No—in fact, I want this feeling—this moment—to last a hundred years. I want this moment to stretch out like a rubber band until it snaps from delirious pleasure, and all of time is frozen in this wonderful night forever. Holt promised me tricks and treats—*fireworks*—and he's delivering far more than that.

Time moves in uneven jags as Holt loves me with his body. My nerves dance on their raw edges in rhythm to his thrusts, shouting with a fury as a fire builds in me that only Holt can quench.

"*Shit*," he whispers as his body slams into mine, harder—faster. Holt is racing to the finish line. His muscles tense over me, solid as sheetrock. I glide my hands down his back and dig my nails into his hips as he gives the last few violent thrusts. Holt lets out a groan and stiffens over my body before giving a mean shudder. He tracks wet kisses to my temple, dripping down to my ear, panting up a storm, making me warm and heady. "You okay?"

"Yes." I find his lips and tear off a kiss. "God, yes." I pull his bottom lip into my mouth and graze it with my teeth, sucking it down, trying to swallow it. "For the first time in my life I feel better than okay." I fall back to the pillow and pant through a smile. "I feel happy. You make me happy, Holt." Tears come without permission. It's true. Holt cut the head off the demons that have haunted me for so long, and I feel whole again.

"You make me happy, Iz." And strangely he looks grieved at the concept.

I take a quivering breath. "So when do we break out the whips and chains?"

Holt rumbles out a laugh before licking a line from my cheek to my ear. "Whenever you're ready, kitten."

"With you I'm always ready. You push me past my comfort zone in a good way. Until a couple of weeks ago, I was only going through the motions. It's you who's teaching me how to live."

"Really?" His smile arches up in a shadow before blooming into something far more vexingly wicked. "Because I'm about to teach you something else."

"Oh, yeah? What's that?"

"The fine art of pleasure." Holt lands his lips over mine, rotating his tongue through my mouth as if he were drilling for oil. He moves his lingual efforts down my cheek, dripping those molten kisses to the nape of my neck, stopping briefly at my collarbone. "Heaven," he whispers. "That's what you taste like." Holt continues his journey down my body, his fingers trickling over my hip. His hand floats to my thigh and flattens over my stomach for a moment before he glides up and cups my breast. Holt offers the world's softest massage, digging his fingers into my flesh ever so slightly. He brings his lips over my nipple and takes a gentle bite. A hard groan comes from the both of us in unison. Holt dives down and loves me right there for a brief stretch of time, and my body enlivens, every nerve in my body stands at attention, trying to fan the flames of this building inferno. Holt and I are already burning for each other with the hottest kind of fire, so bright and consuming there's no extinguishing this blaze. His mouth moves lower still to my belly, and an involuntary quiver ripples through me. A small cry escapes my throat as I pick my head off the pillow, taking in this new sensation.

"How's that feel, kitten?" He buries another soft kiss into my stomach before I can answer.

"Insanely good."

Holt looks up and gives the flash of a smile that ignites the room like a bolt of lightning.

His mouth dives over me again as he twirls his tongue into my belly button, and I tremble with an involuntary laugh.

"Maybe too good," I whisper. "But I'm not complaining." I thread my fingers through his thick, glossy hair. All those weeks I've wanted to do this. Holt has the most amazing soft hair, slick and cool.

He moves his meandering kisses to my waist. Holt traces out the curve of my hip straight down my leg, my shin, then races back up through the inside of my thigh and my legs clamp shut.

"Whoa." He inches back. "No one said tonight was going to end in a decapitation."

"Nor should it." I pull him back up by the arm, and he lands another mouthwatering kiss over my lips. Holt has it backward. He's the one that tastes like heaven. Who knew the best part of my existence would be the day I fell into Holt Edwards' mouth? His *bed*.

"I want to make you feel good."

"You do." I tuck myself beneath him. "You know what I like?"

"Piña coladas and getting caught in the rain?"

"Making love after midnight." I pull him in by the cheeks and feel him growing against my thigh.

Holt reaches over to his nightstand once again.

I think we can go on forever like this.

I think we will.

ଓଓଓଓ

The morning light cuts through my lids like a laser, blinding me, pulling me away from the blissful dream I'm having. Holt and I are on a warm sunny beach, rolling in the sand, losing ourselves in a sea of wild kisses.

Something touches my foot, and I kick it away. Damn cats. A soft wet sensation streams across my stomach, and I squirm in an effort to wriggle my way back into that beachfront fantasy. A warm wet streak sinks down past my hip and into places that cats should never venture.

"God!" I sit up, clutching at a ball of fur that—has Holt Edwards' face attached? "Oh!" I sink back on my elbows as he swims up. "Sorry."

"Morning to you, too." He gives a kiss through his smile. "More like afternoon. It's one-thirty."

"It is not!" I bat his arm before drawing him in.

"God's honest truth." His teeth bump against mine, and I savor the feeling.

"In that case, good morning and good afternoon." I pull his body over me like a blanket.

"Should we go for good evening?"

"As long as you're not starving, I'm good."

"Really? Because while you were catching up on your beauty sleep I snuck over to the kitchen and made you this."

Holt pulls a plate from the nightstand—a tower of pancakes swimming in syrup.

"In that case, I lied." I sit up and pull the sheets to my chest. "I'm absolutely starving."

"Good, because I'm starving, too." Holt plunges his fork into the gooey confection and breaks off a piece. "I'm going to feed you."

"You're going to feed me?" An involuntary purr filters from my throat. He slips the first bite into my mouth—warm and light as air. I give a hard moan. "Mmm—that's perfection. Did you make those? I think you missed your calling."

"I did, and thank you. By the way"—he tilts into me with that sexier-than-hell half drugged look on his face—"it's pretty damn erotic watching you eat."

"Really. Well, you're in luck because it's no rarity. I'm pretty religious about getting three square meals a day. And I'm not shy about it either."

"We've got that in common. Plus, I like to cook."

"So you're saying you're handy both in and out of the bedroom." I wrap my arms around him, giving his bare bottom a squeeze. "You're just one surprise after another. I should have guessed. Those grilled cheese sandwiches were the best I've ever had."

"I figured the only reason you were hanging around was to score another one."

"I did say I'd do anything. Am I close?"

"You're getting there." He feeds me another ultra soft bite—sweet and buttery as sin.

"Mmm. I don't know which I like best. These are pretty darn good."

He lands the plate back on the nightstand and lies over me, hot to the touch. Holt blinks a smile. His eyes glaze over with lust, and that tender spot between my legs spasms.

"I was sort of hoping you'd say you liked this one best." Holt melts an impossibly delicious kiss onto my mouth that far exceeds any common breakfast fare, any grilled meal anyone could ever come up with. Holt is scrumptious on a sublime level. This is the food of the gods. Holt is turning water into wine and delivering the miracle straight to my mouth. The room sways. The bed gives a soft roll as I drink him down, becoming inebriated off our love all over again. Right now the only thing I want to feast on is Holt Edwards' body. I'm already drunk off his affection—addicted to his deep-throated syrup sweet kisses, the heavenly scent of wild musk his skin naturally gives off.

"I changed my mind." I moan as he works his way down my chest. "I definitely like this one best. You win, Holt. You're my favorite meal."

Something cool drips over my stomach and takes my breath away. My eyes spring open to find Holt drizzling syrup straight from the bottle over my bare skin in a large growing circle.

"*You!*" A laugh bubbles from my throat, and I give a weak attempt at pushing him away.

"I thought you might want to sweeten things up." He lands the syrup back on the nightstand before swiping his finger through the gooey mess. "Would you like the first lick?"

I take his finger and plunge it into my mouth like a threat. Holt's eyes widen before he settles into that lewd grin I've grown to crave.

"I like how you think." I skim the syrup off my body and place my hand over that part of him that's most enthused to see me. "I'd like to give you a proper good morning, then we can officially move on to an equally pleasant afternoon, and you won't believe what I have planned to satisfy you this evening."

"I've always pegged you for a sex siren."

"Siren, huh?" Something stirs in me and pushes me further than I thought I could ever go. "How about I make you go off like a siren." I slink down the bed and touch my lips over his sticky sweet body, down past his stomach, past his hips to where he's already saluting my efforts. "Get ready to scream."

Holt is amazingly long, impossibly hard. I'm still stuck on how he could ever fit into my body let alone how he might fit in my mouth. My lips find him, and I take him in, plunging down over and over, ironically drawing on my lesson in the erotic arts from Jemma of all people. I guess her public spectacle of a tutorial had its benefits after all. I can practically hear her scolding me, *no teeth!*

Holt twists my body, pulling my legs toward his lips. He buries a kiss in my stomach, then lower still until his mouth finds me right in that sweet spot that's been secretly waiting for him to do just that.

I pull back and catch my breath a moment before landing my mouth over him again. A blissful eternity stretches by as we take our time getting there. The world spins faster. The room pulsates with a heartbeat all its own as my entire body thumps in rhythm to the universe. Holt and I are weightless, hopelessly lost in our bliss in this new world of our own making. We are levitating to the ceiling—floating right through the beams and into the night. We burn through the sky, and even that is not enough. We're soaring into the stratosphere, swimming through space, racing toward the sun. This is the climax of my entire existence. I never knew it could be this brilliant, that I could feel so explosively alive all at once.

I pull my mouth off him as my body gives way to a violent series of spasms.

"*Holt.*" My skin sizzles with a quake that wakes up every nerve in my body and bathes them in an ecstasy that rails through me like a tuning fork. A warm gush of liquid pulsates over my neck as Holt meets me right there at the finish line.

We clutch onto one another with our feverish bodies, wet and alive with passion as we try to catch our breath.

This is amazing.

And it wouldn't be this wonderful without Holt.

I want to keep him, but a part of me knows I can't.

Holt

Two days straight she stayed. Izzy Sawyer landed her beautiful self in my bed, and I didn't have to resort to five way restraints to keep her there.

Bryson asked if I could meet him at the Ice Bar. It's a good drive, but the next closest bar to the Black Bear as far as the ones that my father owns. The outside of the establishment is painted a crisp blue with a giant plastic glacier sitting on the roof—my mother's doing. I remember how much my father protested the idea. He wanted an overgrown martini glass, but my mother and her ode to the North Pole won out. And then she planted a penguin on that damn block of fake ice as if to prove a point. That pretty much accounts for all the kids we've had wandering into the place looking for the polar exhibit. Maybe not her brightest idea. But then again maybe it was. Maybe it was the big *fuck you* for his infidelity issues.

I stroll into the dim environment. The entire place is cold as a witch's tit. The bar and floors are made of acrylic, but it's frigid as a meat locker in here. There's a special room in back with an ice luge, and, if you're not careful, you can freeze your tongue to your glass. It happens almost nightly because God knows someone has to test out the theory. All of the bartenders are thoroughly trained to deal with any lingual emergencies that might arise. Once, we had a couple try to pull off a quickie, and the idiot sued us for his frost bitten blue balls. People can be dumb as fuck.

I spot Bryson in the back and head on over.

"What's up, baby bro? You forget how to get back home? A little black bird swoop down and gobble up all your bread crumbs?"

"The only bird I see around here is a dodo." He gives a short-lived grin. "Oh, wait, that's you." He smacks me over the arm with his clipboard. "Check this out you moron." He points up to a nice size crack that snakes through the drywall.

"You dragged me out here to watch you do a patch job?"

"Nope. I dragged you out here to help inspect this place from floor to ceiling. Dad says the city is after him. They're sending out inspectors in a couple weeks to detail the place. If we're going to get a loan, we'll need this place to sparkle and shine."

"Back up the train. 'If *we're* going to get a loan?'"

"That's right, sweetheart. Did I stutter? Just because I've got a business degree is no reason to look down upon me." He gives a sheepish grin. "You're right, keeping the bars would be a good decision. And, if you're not too pissed at me, I want to do it with you." He holds out his fist. "You all right with that?"

I give him a quick knuckle bump. "I'm more than all right with that, dude. I am fucking in." I glance around.

"This could be all ours." My sweet baby sis flashes through my mind. "We should figure out a way to include Annie."

"I was thinking the same thing." He nods. "Ryder said he'd get someone from his legal department to write something up for us. An agreement that binds us together in our new business venture."

"Sounds like a solid plan. Maybe that degree of yours is coming in handy after all."

"Maybe it is." He motions over to the nearest table and we take a seat. "I'm sorry, dude. Swear to God, I'll never rub it in your face again. I felt like shit when you left. Still do."

"It's over. It's like it never happened." I lean onto my elbows while taking in my brother. Most of the time it's like looking in a mirror, but that's where the resemblance ends. Bryson is smart. He's way too bright to ever have taken down our family in some stupid move that, in turn, kicked in my own destiny and spun it on its axis. I was the studious one in high school. I'm the one that convinced Bryson we should apply to any, and every, college that might let us in. Hell, we got our acceptance letters to Whitney Briggs the exact same day. But, by that point, I couldn't live with myself. For sure I couldn't focus in on a stack of textbooks. Nope. I was knee deep in emotional vomit and sinking fast.

"So what's going on with you?" Bryson nods like he knows. "Cole says you called in yesterday. You feeling okay?"

A shit-eating grin is dying to break out on my face, so I give.

He shakes his head. "No fucking way."

"Yes fucking way, and watch your language where my girl is concerned."

"Your girl?" He leans in amused. "So this is happening. Does Laney know?"

"I doubt anyone knows." I glance around as if I might accidentally spot Laney here. "She's got this thing." I blow out a breath. "I'm not really sure what it is. But she's definitely got a hang-up about relationships. As far as I know we're unclassifiable, but I'm all right with that." I'm sort of gun-shy to claim a relationship myself—but I'm getting there. "All I know is I don't want anyone else. I want Izzy. She's all I ever wanted."

"I hear that." His brows rise as if he still can't wrap his head around it. "So you're the real deal. Can't wait to tell Baya."

"Dude, were you listening to anything I said? She's skittish when it comes to stuff like that. She's all torn up on the inside. Something serious went down with Izzy, and she's spiraling through the air like a dove with a bullet through her wing."

He leans back and tries to connect with what I'm saying.

"You love her?"

"Yes." I don't hesitate with the answer. "And I'd swear on my life she loves me, too."

183

"Wait a minute. She's that fragile, and I'm assuming the reason for the no-show was because you two were playing honeymoon, but you haven't hit a verbal home run yet?" He ticks his head back a notch as if he's calling bullshit.

"True as God. Every word. She can't say it." I was willing to. Even though it went against everything I thought I stood for. I'm ready to break every rule in the book for Izzy.

"Something is up." He shakes his head. "You think she'll break your heart?"

A sharp sting knifes me in the gut. What if this whole Izzy thing is simply the universe's way of getting back at me? Just some macabre retribution that I've had coming for the last several years. What if I've been looking the Semi in the headlights and mistaken them for Izzy's bright smile? Shit. I close my eyes for a moment. I bet that's what this is. My life doesn't function in fairytale mode like my brother's. According to him, Baya walked right up and flashed her tits. That's how the golden boy gets introduced to the woman of his dreams. Not me—I meet my girl as some sexed up thirteen-year-old with a hard-on at the ready. From there it was girls with daddy issues and barflies galore, hypersexual coeds ready and willing to take me on—nothing but a string of one-night stands because I couldn't stomach the idea of anything lasting longer. Nope never was lucky in the relationship department. Nor should I ever be.

"What's eating you, dude?"

"Nothing's eating me."

"Something is gnawing your balls off. Is it the fact you think she's not in this for the long haul?"

"No. It's not that. This whole thing just got me worked up. I'm just wondering if maybe I should let go of a few of my own issues."

"Now we're getting somewhere." Bryson leans in, stares me down stern as shit. "What the hell happened after high school that threw you in the deep end of the Black Bear that you've yet to recover from?"

"So you were onto me, huh?" A dull laugh rattles from my chest.

"I'd like to say I know you as good as I know myself, but that stopped after senior year. You let me go to Whitney Briggs without so much as a goodbye. I knew were moping but could never figure out why since you were the one who made the decision to sit out the first year. Then it turned into the second year—the third, and now here I am, Mr. Diploma, and you're just as big a mystery as ever." He tilts his head, never taking his eyes off mine. "What gives big bro?"

"You hit all the ducks on the head so far." I snatch up his notebook and stand. "Keep guessing."

I'm not telling.

Not now.

Not ever.

9

All the Dirty Details

Izzy

Dad,

Maybe I'm not as injured as I thought. I may have found a pinhole of light—heck, I know I did. It's bloomed into a super nova, a star that's exploding around me with all of its splendor. Is this what it feels like to fall in love? For the first time ever, I feel like I'm a part of something bigger than myself, bigger than the world, the universe. Who knew this wonderful force existed? Well, most likely everyone else. But as for me—it feels as if I've been reborn.

New again in Hollow Brook,
~Your baby girl

Jemma isn't one to mince words. So when she demands I haul ass to her place ASAP I put on my running shoes and speed over. Usually this sort of distress signal from my BFF kicks off a spontaneous moving day, one in which we pack up her apartment before her soon-to-be ex comes home from the strip club. Lord knows I've helped her clear out a three bedroom in under thirty on more than one occasion. Only, when I walk in, there's not a box in sight. No pile of broken dishes to attest to how pissed off she is, and not a single mound of "his expensive crap" awaiting a trip to the pawnshop. Instead, I find Jemma participating in a rather domestic activity—baking cookies. The kids are all lined up on the couch watching cartoons with their matching trance-like, surprisingly clean, faces.

"Don't judge." She holds out a batter-laden spoon. "One day you'll have an entire herd of rug rats, and you'll wonder how I ever survived with my hair intact. I'm telling you, Sponge Bob makes a damn good babysitter, and he's only one DVR away in a pinch."

"Got it." I find this doubtful. For one, I haven't even considered bringing my own children into this world, and two, my mother—

Then it hits me. I had sex with Holt. It was the exact procreative measure necessary to fulfill such a wish list. My mouth falls opens, and I'm lost for a moment just daydreaming what children with Holt might look like when Jemma jabs me in the chest with her overgrown acrylic nail.

"Knew it," she snickers, grabbing a hold of me by the wrist. I follow her back to the kitchen where she pulls a fresh batch of chocolate chip cookies from the oven. "Spill it, Sawyer. Where, when, what, and, well, I think I know who." She claws the air like a tigress in heat.

"His place, the last two bliss-filled days, everything, and yes—Holt Edwards was the prime suspect." I plop down at the table and shove a hot cookie in my mouth.

"Holy Jezebel." She falls into the seat across from me, slacked jawed and pale. "There are so many miracles that just happened—I think we'd better get Mother Teresa on the line."

"Mother Teresa is dead."

"Then get the freaking Pope!"

"I'm not Catholic. And I hardly think the 'freaking Pope' will give a rat's ass. Relax, would you? Things just sort of progressed with Holt and me, the end. No need to drag religious hierarchy into this."

She gives a solemn nod. "So, did you mention anything about that whole—"

"Nope." I snatch another cookie off the pan. "And I don't think I'm going to. It's not important."

"You think?" Her face contorts in a grimace. "I guess I always thought once you got serious with someone, you'd be able to talk things through. There aren't too many people out there you tell that stuff to. Plus, you know—it's affected you. Don't you think he's picked up on that by now?"

"Picked up on the fact I'm damaged goods? He's a smart boy. I'm sure he's known from the beginning. But, I've sort of skirted the topic each time he's asked. He knows I'm not ready to go there. Besides, if I didn't know better, I'd bet he's got a few hang-ups of his own."

"Oh, hon—I swear over my dead mother's grave that everyone's got a hang up. Maybe that's what makes you two peas in a pod. I bet that weird social juju you carry around like a torch attracted him to you. Moth to a flame." She nods at her tired analogy.

"Please. It did not. Holt says he's been crushing on me since he was thirteen. In fact, that day it happened"—I glance at the tablecloth and pull on a stray fiber—"he was one of the last people I spoke to." The memories rush back like a flood. It was just Holt and me in that stifling studio after the girls ran out to change. I can still see him standing there, looking at me a moment too long, and even then I knew what he was thinking. "He said I was beautiful." Tears blur my vision, and I sniff them back, shoving another cookie in my mouth before they have a chance to surface. I swallow it down as if I were trying to dam up the past. "Jem"—I press my lips in tight—"I think I love him. In fact, I know I do."

"Izzy"—she whispers so low it sounds like a hiss—"those words were meant for sharing." She bears into me with a solemn nod. "The sooner the better." She gets up and pours me a tall glass of milk and pushes the pan in my direction. "So—how was it? Did you walk funny in the morning? 'Cause if you didn't, I hate to break it to you—you did it wrong."

She hedges her hand toward mine, and I'm quick to smack her away.

"Walk funny? I could barely stand. You didn't tell me it would feel like someone scraped me raw with a sanding belt."

"Ooh!" She squeals. "He must be a big one." Jemma starts in with a spontaneous applause.

"Would you stop?" I throw a piece of my cookie at her. "I'm glad you're amused, and, since you asked, yes, he is well-endowed." Not that I would know the difference, but my insides seem to confirm this theory all on their own.

"Anything else?" She gravels it out, rife with sexual pretense. "Does that boy like toys—or was his new pet kitty enough to keep him occupied?"

"No toys. But he does have an affinity for syrup." I clamp my hand over my mouth because I'm about to regret this.

Jemma lets out a whoop and stomps both her hands over the table like she's rooting for the home team, and, in a way, she is.

"I called it!" She howls. "That boy is a freak of nature."

"He is, but in a good way. I'm afraid together we might be just plain freaks." I wrinkle my nose. "I hate that I'm older than him."

"You're insane."

"No, really. It sort of bugs me. I mean not when we're together. I don't even notice it. But I wonder if other people do. Is that weird?"

"Yes, and I think we've already established the fact you're weird in general, so get over it. You're the new *it* couple. You're the couple of the new millennium. You're like Ashton and Demi."

"Newsflash Ashton and Demi aren't together anymore. He's currently with a much younger woman."

"So sue me. I've got kids and live under a Dora-shaped rock." She leans in like a tiger about to pounce. "So you sharing? Or is this one going on the private reserve list."

"No, I'm not sharing."

"Sharing is caring."

God, she's drooling now.

"Creating STDs does not say you care. Holt is mine, back off, Jem. Besides, aren't you off the market?"

She blows out an unsteady breath. "Ron says he wants to see other people."

"See? As in *see* other people?"

"As in see what they have to offer under the hood, take 'em for a test drive—you know the drill—try out another model." She picks up a cookie and taps it over the table. "But I guess I'm okay with it." She shakes out her blonde curls, and they catch the light streaming in from the window. I've always admired her lemon waves. In fact, I've always admired everything about Jemma, but, lately, her life just looks hard—three kids, almost just as many husbands under her belt, and now this new arrangement. I don't think I could handle it if Holt were seeing other people on the side.

"How are you okay with this?" I'm afraid to tread in this direction. I can tell by the crumbling look of grief on her face that she's not okay with any of it.

"I don't know. I think maybe it's time to settle down and find me a sugar daddy." She blinks a quick smile. "God knows I'm going to need one. Denny hasn't paid child support in two months. If this keeps up, I'll be needing a J-O-B, and the only J-O-B I'm currently skilled at has the word blow in front of it." Her expression sours. "Hey, you think Holt needs a new waitress at the bar?"

"It's not that kind of bar." My lips twist. "I'm teasing. I'll ask."

"Thanks. That way I can pull double duty and catch me one of those cute frat boys like you did. We can start our own sorority—the Cougar Club. *Rawr!*" She claws the air, and suddenly I'm fearing for my eyes and my social standing.

"We're not old enough to qualify as cougars." I hope.

"You just keep believing that. And if anyone gives you any shit. You tell them you've got an entire den of crazy cats just waiting to pounce."

"Crazy cats." That sounds about right.

Lila rushes in and snatches a cookie off the table.

"Hey, that's not fair!" She scolds through a laugh. "You guys ate all the cookies!"

"Come here, you." Jemma scoops her up and plants a sweet kiss on top of her little blonde head.

"Hey girl!" I give her finger a quick tug. "When are you coming to dance for me?"

"I gonna go when my momma tells me." She smears the cookie over her mouth like lipstick.

"Good girl." Jemma buries another kiss in her hair before making crazy eyes at me. I know how Jemma feels about the financial commitment that goes along with the studio. It's anything but cheap. The monthly tuition can easily equate to a small car payment.

"How about I comp this one?" I give a little wink.

"Your mother will shit a brick the size of a refrigerator."

Sometimes I think Jemma knows my mother better than I do.

"She won't have to. I'm thinking of taking over the studio. She wants to sell."

Jemma sucks in a never-ending breath. "Are you shitting me? I would have thought she'd keel over in that place before she ever gave it away. What's the story?"

"Greasy D was up to his old tricks, so I told him to take a hike. He took off, and now she's blaming the studio for her inability to hang onto a 'damn man.'"

"Selling it over a damn man." She mindlessly picks up a cookie with her gaze fixed on a faraway horizon. "I wonder what she would do if she found out it was you all along?"

I wonder the exact same thing.

ഇാര

That afternoon Laney sends a text and lets me know there's a fitting at the bridal shop. I drive all the way to downtown Jepson with its metropolitan appeal, its skyscrapers—and a twinge of envy bites through me. Laney really does have it all. And I'm thrilled that Ryder is not only one of the nicest guys on the planet, but he's established in life, too. I'd hate to see her in the same position as Jemma. Poor thing. I worry for her sanity almost as much as I do mine. But then I'm no Laney, either. I've got issues I could stack to the moon myself.

I wonder how different my life would have been if that day never happened? If I would have found someone to talk to—someone who could have helped me move beyond the hellish borders of that night. Instead, I cemented my emotional feet in it and spent the next decade holding the rest of the world at bay. I wonder how different things would be—how far I could have gotten in life by now—if my father had just stuck around in the first place.

The posh bridal shop comes up on my right, and I park and hop out.

I wonder if I would have long since met my Mr. Right and had a few kids of my own by now. Would I still be at the studio? My head spins with the possibilities.

Holt comes to mind with his hotter-than-a New York-sidewalk-in-July smile, those teeth that flash bright as a North Carolina sunrise each time he opens his mouth. Holt is a god among men and deserves to be venerated as such. I'm sure there are plenty of coeds ready and willing to drop to their knees for him. I wonder if I'm nothing more than some fantasy conquest left over from his childhood. But I don't think I am. I can feel a real connection between us. Holt and I are on the path to something great if we ever let it get there.

I step inside the overpriced dress shop, and the scent of spiced tea hits me, thick and suffocating. An entire sea of white candles glow along a granite counter. The facility alone is large enough to outfit an entire fleet of honeymoon bound 747s.

Baya waves from the main room, and I make my way past countless bridal parties as they fawn over their own brides in the making.

"Where's Laney?" I give her a quick hug before joining Annie and Roxy on the white velvet sofa.

"Trying on her dress." Roxy hammers it out devoid of any emotion. Roxy has had the same hardcore personality since she was a kid. She's consistent, I'll give her that.

"Have you seen it?" Baya bounces in her seat so hard that the entire sofa shakes with her Richter scale exuberance.

"No, but I'm dying to." I've invested more than Laney will ever know to make sure she gets her happily ever after.

Annie pulls out her phone and jots something down before flashing it at me.

Baya says you're seeing my brother.

I bite my lip and resist the urge to smile.

"I don't know, am I?" I shrug, and give a little laugh.

Annie is quick to type out a reply.

Are you coming to my Mom's birthday party tomorrow night? She's turning 50. It's a pretty big deal. I'll be cooking. I promise, it won't kill you. I'm actually getting better in the kitchen.

I give a little smile. My stomach cinches. I'm not sure Holt and I are at that phase in our non-relationship, but a part of me wants him to ask. I'll be seeing him later. Maybe he will.

"That would be nice." My throat dries out at the thought. A family party is the exact kind of thing that couples do. "But he hasn't really mentioned it."

I'm sure he will. She gives a sheepish smile. **I'm glad you're with Holt. I think you're cute together.**

"Thank you. I'm glad I'm with Holt, too." There, the words slipped out like oil, and I didn't cringe or explode into a thousand remorseful pieces. Maybe it's okay for me to say those words—to feel that way.

Annie drops her phone and cups her hands over her mouth. Roxy gasps, and Baya jumps to her feet. I turn to find Laney—stunning, beautiful Laney—heading in this direction.

"Oh my, God." The words stream from me in a deflated whisper. I stand to greet her and take up her hands. She's wearing a full white gown with layers of tulle and a sweetheart neckline. "You are a princess, through and through." Tears spring to my eyes, and I don't fight them.

Laney beams as she steps up on the pedestal. She does a quick rotation in the three way mirror and presses her lips together because she's about to lose it herself.

"Your turn, Baya." She wipes her face down as Baya makes her way to the back.

"Laney, I can't tell you enough how beautiful you look," I say, trying to compose myself.

"It's true. You look like the perfect cake topper," Roxy pipes up. "I'm just glad you're letting me wear black. Come to think of it, I'll probably wear black to my own wedding."

"You throwing your hat in the ring?" Laney glances at herself in the mirror from over her shoulder.

"No way," Roxy is quick to set her straight. "Cole and I are waiting until after graduation." She turns to me. "We plan on hitting the ground running with our own businesses. He's doing construction, and I'm opening a bakery."

"Sounds like I'll be visiting you a lot."

Her eyes widen as Baya comes out. Baya stuns in a sleek mermaid gown with a full train and just enough sparkle to catch the light. She heads over to Laney and clasps her arms around her waist.

"You both look amazing." They look like jewels, like treasures, and they are.

Annie, Roxy, and I each try on our bridesmaid dresses. Roxy and Annie both look gorgeous in the gowns they've chosen.

The dress Laney hand selected for me is long with a rhinestone-encrusted waist and a plunging neckline that showcases my own jewels. I have to admit I look pretty damn good, but it's a far cry from the matronly number I picked out for myself. In a way, I guess, the two dresses are symbolic of the lost girl I was and the woman slowly emerging in me. Holt pulled me from the mud and mire of the past. He's washing me anew with his love. And now I can't wait for him to see me in this dress—and then out of it.

I wrap an arm around Laney as we look in the mirror.

"It's going to be a perfect day," I whisper.

Baya, Roxy, and Annie head back to change and Laney picks up both my hands.

"Baya hinted that things are getting pretty serious between you and Holt."

I try to look away, but Laney catches my gaze and doesn't let go.

"Maybe—yes." Crap. "So I guess Holt told Bryson, and the rest is Whitney Briggs rumor mill history."

"Not true." She touches her finger to my chin. "I asked. I'm the one that probed. And, yes, Holt told his brother, but they're close." Laney lets my fingers slip through hers.

"I think we're close."

"Are we?" She inches forward as if she's about to whisper a secret. "If we're so close, why is there something big I don't know about, Izzy? And if that's true, are you ever going to tell me?"

The temperature in the room feels as if it spikes fifty degrees, and the dress suddenly feels three sizes too small. I breakout in a cold sweat and the floor begins to sway.

"You know"—I touch my hand to my forehead—"I'm not feeling so hot. I think I'd better go."

I make a dash for the dressing room. The last thing I want to do is tell Laney every dirty detail right before her wedding. I've managed to protect her this far, and I'll be damned if I don't make it to the finish line.

If I get my way, the finish life will be my grave.

Holt

The Black Bear feels like home. It feels like family—sometimes closer than a brother.

It's wall-to-wall bodies as the sorority girls pour in to witness another round of house band prospects.

"Why don't we give it to three or four bands?" I say to Bryson as he plucks his phone from his jeans. He's studiously jotting down notes as each band performs.

"We could rotate." Cole nods into the idea.

"Because the band we heard last night sounded like an engine dying a slow death," he says, irritated as shit. "Besides, we still have karaoke night and a DJ on Fridays. I don't think we should clog up every night of the week."

"Good point."

The band starts up, and I think every animal in a twenty-foot radius just ran for cover. "Crap." It's all I can do to keep from slapping my hands over my ears. "Keep looking, dude. I can tell from go this one ain't it."

A gorgeous brunette walks in, and my dick perks to attention.

Izzy gives me that heart-stopping smile, and I magnetize toward her.

"Hey, good looking." I stop shy of stealing a kiss. Even though there's a sea of people around too busy to notice, I'm still not sure she'd be into it.

"You redefine good looking." She runs her finger along my jawline. "Any chance of getting off early?"

She looks hopeful. Izzy has on a little black dress that hugs her in all the right places, and heels that almost bring her to my height. She grinds her hips into mine, and my dick springs out to greet her.

"I'm getting off right now, kitten." I lean in and stop myself from burying my face in her neck. Izzy holds the scent of honey and lavender. "But as for this place, I've got at least another hour. It's Cole's turn to close." I take her in again from head to foot. "Damn, you are looking hot tonight."

Izzy cuts a sly look across the crowd. "Too bad there's not a minute we can steal to be alone." She twists her lips and gets a mischievous look in her eye. "You know, so I can help you get off—wherever it is you'd like to go."

Holy hell. I think I've just been propositioned.

Without giving it a second thought, I take her by the hand and lead her through the crowd—straight to the women's restroom. I've seen this done enough times to know how it works. Last stall on the left might as well be on Jupiter.

There's not a soul in sight, so I steal us away to the back and lock the door.

The speakers are on overhead, and you can't hear yourself think straight in here, just the way I like it.

"I've missed you," I whisper right into her ear.

Izzy lands those pillow-soft lips over my cheek and rakes a trail to my mouth.

"I've missed you, too." She strums the words right into my lips.

I cup her cheeks in my hands and set her lips on fire with mine. Izzy gives soft, soulful kisses—kisses that stretch out for weeks. This is exactly what I want the rest of my life to be like—nothing but Izzy pouring her addictive kisses right down my throat. Izzy is a dessert I've longed for, and, now, here she is with her sweet body pressed over mine right where she belongs.

She gently pulls my hands down onto her hips. I ride a little lower still until I hit the hem on her short-as-hell dress and touch her bare thighs beneath that. She takes a quick breath and seizes against me. Her hands travel down my chest, right to my blooming hard-on, and she's quick to unleash it from its denim prison.

"You want to do this?" I take a gentle bite out of her earlobe and she shivers into me.

"We're doing it aren't we?" She gives a little laugh as she peppers soft kisses down my neck, giving me a little bite of her own. "You in?"

"Not only am I in"—I pluck the condom out of my pocket and give a little grin— "I come prepared."

"*Ooh*." Her eyes widen for a moment. "I'm digging the double entendre."

"And I'm digging you speaking French." I crash my mouth to hers and lose it. Her tongue lashes over mine like a punishment. I ease her against the door and work her dress up, pulling her underwear to the side.

Izzy helps me roll on the rubber before I lift her onto my hips.

She touches her hand to my face and pants through a crooked smile.

"*Iz*." I bear into her in lieu of saying those three magic words that have the power to send her running out of here like a bullet. Her lids grow sleepy. Her lips bloom full and ruby. Izzy looks drugged, lost in ecstasy, exactly how I imagined she would look if we ever got around to doing this—how I hoped she would look.

Izzy sinks down over me, and her head arches back. She bites down onto her lip with her eyes shut tight as if she's enjoying the hell out of it—at least I hope she is.

I suck in a quick breath as I lower her over my body. Izzy digs her fingers into my shoulders and buries her face in my neck.

"*Holt*," she gives it in a heated whisper.

"I got you." I plunge her over me, again and again, until I'm almost there. She takes everything I'm giving her, moaning softly in my ear, saying my name until it drives me insane. "Izzy, I—" I almost said it. I don't know if I can keep the words from flying out of my mouth.

I give about three more thrusts and lock her body down over mine. Neither of us moves as I give in to my release. I throb for days, shaking out deep inside her as I bury my face in her hair.

"That was heaven," I whisper. "Sorry—I was greedy." I press a kiss into the hollow of her neck. "Spend the night. Let me make it up to you."

She tilts back and belts out a laugh. "Maybe I will."

"You want to hang out? I'll entertain the hell out of you with my mixer moves."

"Sounds like a plan."

"Then maybe we can catch a movie. Or there's always tomorrow night." I take a quick breath. "Mmm." I wince as Mom's birthday comes to mind. "I just remembered I've got this family thing tomorrow night, but hey, there's always Sunday, right?"

"A family thing?" She nods into me expectantly. Izzy is so damn beautiful she looks like Ms. America 24/7, never mind the fact she's got that I've-just-been-fucked look that's making me insane. But I'm not sure about bringing her to any family thing just yet.

I dot her cheek with a kiss. "It's not important." As much as I want to bring Izzy home, I can't stomach the thought of flaunting my new relationship in front of my mother after what I did to her. I don't think I can go there just yet—ever maybe.

"Not important, huh?" Her features soften. Izzy sags in my arms, dejected. "That's fine." She gives a sad smile. "And you know what? I totally get it." She hops down and readjusts her dress.

We head back out into the bar, and she glances at her phone.

"It's my mom. I think I'd better head out. She twisted her ankle a few weeks back."

"Will I see you tonight?" I run my fingers through her hair, afraid I might have hurt her somehow. It's written all over her face that I did.

"We'll see." She gives a little shrug and heads out the door.

I've been around enough girls to know I'm in the doghouse.

I just can't figure out why.

§⊙§

Saturday night rolls around and still no sign or word from Izzy. I know she mentioned her mother needed her, but it's pretty clear that was just an excuse. Baya and Bryson drive out to my mother's together, and I hop in my truck and head over alone. I should've asked Izzy to come. It would have been the perfect time to introduce her to my mother. My stomach knots up as if protesting the idea.

I park and head on up. Annie has the house decorated with streamers and balloons. A large banner is strung out over the living room that reads *Happy Birthday Mom! 50 years young!*

Mom is in the den, already chatting it up with Baya and Bryson.

"It's the birthday princess." I pull her into a nice, tight hug and give her cheek a little peck. "Happy birthday. You look great."

"So do you." She gently slaps my cheeks before looking over my shoulder. "Alone are we?"

"As always." It feels right saying that and, yet, a part of me doesn't want it to.

"Annie mentioned you might be bringing someone." She smooths my collar. "I did too with the way you were kissing that girl the night of the engagement party." She lifts her glass as if she were toasting me.

"I sort of thought you were bringing someone, too." Baya shoots me the stink eye.

Annie pops up from behind and signs, *Where's Izzy?*

"I don't know." I sign the words as well, and it feels just as lousy declaring it in two languages. "I'll probably catch up with her later."

I thought she'd be here. Her features sag. Annie looks downright crestfallen that Izzy's not with me. *I told her I was cooking something special. I guess I'll have to wait to show off my culinary skills.* She makes a face.

Crap. Izzy knew about the party. No wonder her mood downshifted when I told her it wasn't anything important. She knew it was.

A young blonde appears next to Annie.

This is my friend, Marley. Annie gives her a half-hug. *She's my new roommate at Whitney Briggs. We move in the day after the wedding.*

"Nice to meet you."

207

Annie used to tutor kids in sign language after school, so she rarely drops the syntax when signing. She's always been a stickler for going the extra mile in everything she does, including expanding her social circle.

"I know you!" The blonde bounces on her heels. "You're that hot bartender at the Black Bear."

"No, that's him." I mock shoot Bryson.

"Nope, it's you." She gives a little wink, and now I'm really wishing Izzy was by my side. Maybe it's not too late to text her. But then it's dark as shit and almost impossible to get here unless you know the way. Maybe I'll surprise her and stop by her place tonight, bring some whiskey and my tail between my legs.

Annie herds us all to the table, and Marley lands across from me with a dreamy look in her eyes.

Perfect.

Baya and Bryson fill the conversation with talk of their wedding. Still can't believe he's getting hitched in just a couple of weeks.

"How about you, Holt?" Mom waves her fork in my direction before taking a bite. "You think you'll be taking the plunge anytime soon?" She tilts her head as if demanding an answer.

"Don't know. I always thought I'd sort of be the forever bachelor." And that's the truth.

"Give him a break." Bryson wads up his napkin and tosses it at me. "He needs to sink his teeth into a relationship first."

"He's just a late bloomer." Mom comes to my defense. "Besides, there are still plenty of options out there for him." She raises her brows in Marley's direction.

Nope. Not going there. I've got all of my options narrowed down to one—the perfect one. I don't need anyone else. I just need Izzy.

"Speaking of relationships, I have an announcement." Mom leans in like a giddy schoolgirl. "I'm back in the dating pool."

Bryson growls at the news. "Tell 'em you got two buff dudes looking out for you."

Baya leans in. "I think it's great. I hope you have a good time."

I lift a glass. "To Mom on what I predict to be the best half of her life." Everyone joins in on the toast. "And to Bryson and Baya. Here's to the happily ever after you both deserve."

We touch glasses and knock back our drinks.

"To happily ever after," Mom chimes.

Sounds like Mom is ready to move on. Grief coats me like lead from the inside out.

My mood plummets, and, as soon as we have cake, I make up an excuse about the bar and hightail it out of there.

Someday soon I'll have to let go of all this bullshit.

Too bad I can't figure out how.

10

All of Me

Izzy

Hi Daddy,

Just when I thought I had my life squared away, the bottom falls out again. That's what I get for leaping into the oily black lie that is love. I loved you. I leaped in your arms every day screaming those very words, and, now, all that's left is a void—dead empty space, brokenness, and whiskey, and my splintered heart. It's a shame I ever trusted anyone—beginning with you.

Maybe I'm not the fuck up—maybe you are,
~Elizabeth

Spending Saturday night with my mother has never really bothered me—until now. I've got the ritualistic chick flick going. We've each washed and set our hair in rollers. I've plied both our faces with enough avocado and raw egg to make any omelet jealous. Our fingers and toes are freshly painted a raucous shade of fuchsia as we watch a waning romantic comedy we've seen at least a dozen times before, but, deep down, I still wish I was with Holt at the birthday party I wasn't invited to.

A gentle knock vibrates from the door, and we freeze.

I cinch my bathrobe shut and look to my mother. "You expecting someone?"

"Nope. You?"

I avert my eyes. "It's almost ten-thirty. Everyone knows that only serial killers and booty calls come a knocking this late." I bat her away. "Get the gun."

"We don't have a gun." She narrows in on me with that are-you-shitting-me look on her face. Mom isn't one to fear anything or anyone—a genetic trait that obviously skips a generation—or at least me.

"Then, obviously, we should *get* one," I hiss. "Call 911."

Her mouth squares out. "So they can do what? Act as a butler service at tax payers' expense?" She waves me off as she heads toward the commotion. "You ever call the cops for something so ridiculous, you're going to end up on the news. It won't be flattering. It's probably just Laney. She's forever losing her key."

"I can count on one hand how many times she's been here this year and still have four fingers and a thumb left over." I jump to my feet in the event I need to smash someone's head in with a lead crystal vase—even though we're currently deficient in such luxuries.

"Smart ass." She flings open the door and her glossy green face brightens. Great, it's probably Donny coming back with his greasy tail between his legs. For his sake he'd better have my forty-five bucks on hand. "Oh look, it's another smart ass!" She widens the door and waves the said *smart ass* in. It's probably Jemma. "Aren't you the margarita mixer who was sucking face with my daughter a few weeks back?"

Oh. My. God.

Holt walks into the room, and our eyes connect in that deer-in-the-headlights kind of way. Mine because he sees me in this hideous slumber party getup, and his most likely because he's pondering how fast he should run away from the two green aliens standing before him.

A smile spreads over his face, wide as the sea.

Somebody kill me.

Here I am, looking like a day spa cast off while the most handsome man in the history of the world stands before me smiling like a loon. God, he's probably laughing—*affirming* to himself it was a brilliant idea not to include me in on his mother's big birthday bash. He's probably here to tell me we're not a good fit, that he prefers dating girls who can't see thirty on the horizon for another ten years. Oh, hell, what do I care—it's not like I don't already have egg on my face.

"So what do you think, Izzy?" Mom plants her fists over her hips. "How would you classify this? Is he a serial killer or is this a—how did you phrase it? *Booty* call?" A grin spreads over her face. "I don't think they call it that anymore." She turns to Holt. "What are the kids calling it these days? A bump and grind? A late night sex summons? Or just a good-old fashioned mounting?"

"Shit," I whimper, dashing past the two of them and throwing myself in the shower. If ever there were a day I could shrivel up and slip down the drain, this one would be nice.

Booty call. I rake a brush through my hair and change into my red silk robe. Is it wrong of me to secretly wish it were Greasy D and not Holt?

I head back out to the living room where my mother is busy staring him down.

Holt has his hair slicked back, a crisp white dress shirt on with his inky dark jeans, and, holy hell, I've never been so glad it's not Greasy.

"Izzy!" My mother sings while patting the spot on the couch beside her. All four cats sit at attention and glare openly at Holt. Honest to God, I've never seen them so riveted by anyone. Bashful looks like he's about to knife him. "I'm so glad you could join us." Mom bubbles with laughter, and it sets off all sorts of alarms inside me. My mother never bubbles. "Your special visitor and I have been getting to know one another." Her voice reaches a melodic crescendo.

Crap. She's never this giddy. Giddy is against her religion. Sarcasm is the altar at which she worships. And if she's not aiming her cynicism in poor Holt's direction—that must mean I'm the one being tied to a stake. Shit. She's about to make an offering to the god of shame and humiliation—and I'd bet the forty-five dollars I no longer have that the sacrifice involves me. "Izzy Sawyer—come *on* down!" She sings as if I've just won a spot on a game show. The Wheel of Misfortune.

I spear her with a look. I swear, that woman has sung her last chorus.

"Holt and I were just going over your old report cards." She fans herself with a stack of white papers.

I suck in a quick breath.

He shakes a small black box, and its contents clatter happily.

"And baby teeth!" She sings over to him.

"My report cards...*baby teeth*?" Fuck.

On second thought I wish I had 911 on speed dial to keep me from killing my mother.

I touch my hands to my temples. Shit, shit, shit! Brain hurts. A serious cerebral injury is taking place, and it's all my mother's fault.

"Report cards, really?" I moan.

"Oh, just high school dear." Mom flicks her wrist on her way over to me. She leans in and kisses my cheek on her way out of the room. "If you kids don't mind, I've got a date with a hunk of steel named Magnum. He's locked, loaded, and ready to go. I've got a thirty-day warranty and

215

brand new D batteries. I'm going to make the best of it."
She glances back at Holt. "It's time to say hello to my little
friend."

Oh. My. God. I close my eyes a moment. I don't
know which is worse. The fact Holt has seen me decked
out like a thirteen-year-old at a sleepover or the fact my
mother just referenced her vibrator in her best Cuban
accent.

Holt appears by my side, and I can't seem to scrape
my gaze off the floor.

"Hey, beautiful." He touches his finger to my chin
and gently lifts it until I'm swimming in those silver
beams he calls eyes. "Brought you something." He
produces a rectangular amber bottle from behind his
back.

"Whiskey?" I jump a little when I say it, mostly
because I think I'm overdue for a good inebriation.

Holt smolders into me—his lids heavy with desire,
and my panties beg to melt right off. Then I remember
where I am and who's in the next room pulling her love
slave out of a box, and my thighs cinch shut.

Okay. I take a breath. Stay calm. This is not a
problem. I'm a grown woman. Who the hell cares if my
mother is home cuddling up to a robotic device in the
name of her warranty? A tiny voice in the back of my head
says me, but I'm quick to squelch it.

"Sorry I didn't call." He leans in and tucks his face in
my neck for a moment.

"I'm not." I touch my hand to the stubble peppering his cheeks and groan. "I'm just glad you're here."

"I want to apologize for not inviting you to my mother's party. It was stupid of me. Believe me, Iz, I can't wait to bring you home. I want you in every part of my life. I swear you're everything—"

I shake my head and touch a finger to his lips.

"I don't need an apology." I pull him in by the back of the neck. "I just need, you." I hike up on my tiptoes and press a gentle kiss against his lips, so chaste and soft, like a butterfly brushing its wings. Here I am, kissing Holt Edwards right in the living room I grew up in. This is going to make a great story to tell all those imaginary future Edwards one day. For sure it trumps Laney's I-met-him-in-the-ladies-room-because-he-forgot-his-contacts anecdote. My mother thought Ryder was a pervert for at least a year.

"I couldn't get here fast enough." He pulls back and whispers over my lips. "You're all I think about. Every second we're not together feels empty. I would have crawled here if I had to."

"Holt." I close my eyes for a moment because a part of me wanted to hear exactly that. I clear my throat and take a deep breath. "So"—a smile bounces on my lips—"you had a chance to spend some time with my mother." I cringe at the thought. What was I thinking leaving him alone in the same room with her? I should have dragged him off to the shower with me. Hindsight is 20/20.

"I like your Mom. She's pretty nice, and I respect her honesty."

"She has no filter." Like less than zero.

"Those are some of my favorite people. Besides, she did nothing but rave about you. She really impressed me." His lips crimp as if he's holding back a laugh. His dimples go off, and that sweet spot between my legs cries out for him. "Of course, I wasn't too impressed with the D you got in algebra. Or that F in chemistry."

Ugh. My mother always said those kind of grades came back to haunt you, obviously I had no idea she would be acting as the poltergeist delivering the news to my newly minted boyfriend.

I touch my fingers to my mouth as if I'd just said that out loud. I guess I sort of do have a boyfriend. I give Holt a little smile as I lead him toward the hall.

"You ready for the grand tour?" I run my tongue over my lips like an afterthought, and his eyes widen. "It ends in my private boudoir."

"Are you kidding? I get to see Izzy Sawyer's bedroom? I've waited nine long years for this moment."

A hard thump comes from my mother's room. "I heard that!"

I avert my eyes at her muffled cry.

"Don't worry. We'll be two whole rooms away." I give a quick wink leading him deeper down the hall, and a horrid rumble shatters the silence as if she's just fired up a lawnmower.

"Oh, Magnum—yes baby, *please!*" She belts it out at the top of her lungs, and the hideous drilling noise gets progressively louder.

"Ignore her," I say, turning the knob to my bedroom. I give the place a quick onceover. I was in such a damn hurry to get back to the living room, I forgot all about the errant bras and panties that might be lying around. God forbid he sees what really goes on underneath my clothes.

"All clear?" He whispers directly into my ear, and a shiver runs up my spine. Holt has the power to melt my bones simply with the sound of his voice.

"All clear." I pull him in by the waist as he glances around the tiny cube of a bedroom. "Just a dresser and a bed."

"Sounds like one piece of furniture more than we'll be needing." Holt presses into me with those heavy glazed eyes. I doubt he notices there are walls in the room let alone furniture. It's pretty clear the only thing he's interested in is me. And I'm damn glad about it.

I pull him over to the mattress, and we sit across from one another as I unscrew the cap on the whiskey.

"I think we should play a game," I say. "I take a hit and tell you something about myself and then you do the same." I want to know everything about Holt, beyond the obvious. Holt has me captive in ways I didn't think were possible. I want to crawl inside his mind and see what makes him tick. He's a good person, sensible and gorgeous, but I've always known those things. I want to linger in the shadows of the deepest darkest part of him and see what makes him the person he is today. And if I'm right, there's something lurking back there that he's not so eager to share. I guess we have that in common. And, in some small way, I'm opening the door for him to find things out about me as well. Although I doubt he knows the right questions to ask. Hell, I hardly know those.

He inches back, inspecting me with a playful curiosity. "I like this game."

My lips meet the edge of the bottle, and I take a smooth drag.

"Whew!" I give a violent shudder as the burn trails down to my stomach. "That's some good stuff. Strong as gasoline."

His dimples flash as he leans in. "You drink gasoline often?"

"Only when my mother tries to offend the boys I'm dragging to my bedroom."

His brows arch in amusement. I think we both know he's the only male who's ventured through that door since, well, ever.

"Okay, I'll go first. I was once the captain of the West Hollow Brook cheerleading squad but got kicked off just before the last game for getting high behind the bleachers." Jemma was involved in that fiasco, but, then, she was present for just about every other fiasco in my scholastic career, so I don't see why not.

"You?"

"That would be me. Your turn."

He takes the bottle from me with that I'm-going-to-bed-you look in his eyes and a quiver erupts between my legs. Holt Edwards has me trembling for him at the drop of a smile. Who ever thought another person could have so much power over me?

Holt throttles the neck and takes a few good swigs.

He lands the bottle on his knee as his shoulders lift a second. "Seventh grade. I once got kicked out of the mall for running away with a shoe. In my defense, it was on a dare, and I willingly gave it back."

"Just one shoe? That's not practical."

His brows swoop low giving him that demonically sexy look that has me spinning with or without any alcohol.

"Nothing about me is practical, Iz."

"Are we practical?" I think I'm ready for that bottle again.

"Do we have to be?" He slides over the whiskey, and I take a quick sip.

"Can I ask you a question?"

"Maybe." I feel it coming like an animal senses an earthquake rumbling, long before the tremor ever hits the surface.

Holt digs into me with those unearthly pale eyes. "What has you running scared?"

And there it is. I take another bitter hit from the bottle, and let the fire race all the way down to my gut.

"So—you want all of my secrets on a platter." I blink a smile as the room starts to sway. "You tell me yours—I'll tell you mine." I've long since suspected Holt has been harboring his own issues.

Holt takes the bottle and indulges in one last swig before settling it between his legs. He looks over with a devilish grin, and suddenly I'm very damn thirsty for whiskey.

"Why do I feel like you're changing the subject?" I reach down and cradle the bottle, letting my fingers graze over the blooming hardness in his jeans. "Hello there." I glance down as I move the whiskey to the nightstand.

"He can't quite hear you."

"Maybe I'd better bring my mouth a little closer." I run my tongue over my bottom lip and the smile slopes right off his face. "Secrets?"

"How about we focus on the here and now?" He scoots over and pulls me onto his lap. His breath warms my neck with the strong scent of whiskey. When I was little, I would open that old bottle my mother keeps as a shrine and take in its scent. It always reminded me of fresh cut wood, of a forest, a man, but oddly never of my father.

Holt holds the scent of a country meadow, earthy and raw. His fingers dig into my flesh as he massages his way up my thighs. I roll my head and give a soft groan until it feels as if I'm falling right through him. Holt and I don't need liquor. We can get drunk simply off each other. Holt is the only high I'll ever need.

"I'm sort of liking the here and now." My heart thumps, wild and rabid as it tries to break free from its cage. I reach up and run my fingers over his rough stubble. Holt is handsome as hell, kind, and I'm pretty sure he'd kill for me. He's my pot of gold, that's for sure. I wonder if he'd want to live in this room with me forever. How could I ever explain that those were the terms I promised my father, but, more so, that I'm the reason my mother would be alone forever—that I could never abandon her to that fate after she sacrificed so much for Laney and me.

"What's running through your mind?" He smears my lips with a juicy kiss.

"I'm thinking you should stay right here in this bed and never leave." I blow the words right over his lips. "You in?"

"I'm in." Holt lies over me, and my robe opens voluntarily.

"There's something I want to give you," I whisper as my heart fires in my chest like a gunshot.

"What's that?" He traces my lips examining me like this, naked and splayed beneath him.

"All of me."

He sighs as a broken smile emerges.

"That's exactly what I want to give you."

I reach over and turn off the light. It feels good like this with Holt. We've crossed some imaginary bridge— hand in hand, we traversed the thorns from the past and made it to a whole new world that we're free to discover together.

Holt glides my panties down, and I pull off his shirt until his bare skin lies over mine like a blessing. This is something I never want to lose, this feeling right here with Holt—my Holt—my boyfriend.

"I hope you brought a suit of armor for your not-so-little friend." I graze my teeth over his neck.

"For you, kitten?" A quiet laugh rumbles from his chest. "I brought the whole damn missile defense system."

"Good because you're going to need it." I trail my hand up his chest, clipping my fingers under his chin. "You didn't plan on getting any sleep tonight, did you, cowboy?"

"Are you kidding? There's no way in hell I'm catching a wink during this rodeo."

"Mmm." I shake my head. "Why do I get the feeling I was just compared to steer? By the way, all cattle-related nicknames are off the table," I tease.

He pulls back with a grimace. "You're definitely no steer." Holt leans up on his elbow examining me with nothing but a wash of moonlight streaming in. "I met all of your cats tonight. You're a real life Snow White—I can call you Snow for short." He sinks a lingering kiss over my lips.

"You can't call me Snow because I'm sort of stuck on kitten." I give an audible purr. "But if I were Snow, that'd make you my prince."

"I'll gladly be a prince for you," he whispers right over my mouth. "*Kitten.*"

Holt glides his mouth up and down my body in long, hot tracks. I unbutton his jeans, and he's quick to shake them off. He holds up a condom, and I help roll it on. I wrap my legs around his back like I'm giving his ribcage a hug as he slowly pushes his way inside. Holt kneads my hips while thrusting his body into mine. Our lips crush together, hard and feverish, as he tries to put out the fire in my mouth with his urgent kisses.

There's no stopping the two of us. This is a runaway rodeo. We've become the fated royal couple, galloping off into the sunset. We roll around on my bed like tigers on fire, like bears fighting to survive in the wild. There's a war brewing beneath the sheets. Something so fantastic is blooming to life that neither of us can quite classify its extraterrestrial beauty.

We tear through the night without any apologies while the headboard drums against the wall with the rhythm of our love.

Holt is no electric gadget built to please. I have the real deal, right here in my bed. And, now that I've tasted paradise, I'm pretty damn sure I never want to leave.

I think I finally found my way out of the maze I've been drifting in for the last solid decade of my life.

Holt led me out of the wasteland—and here we are, rolling around in greener pastures.

Holt Edwards is paradise found. Too bad there's an elephant in the room that neither of us are willing to cop to. I wonder how long before the life is stomped out of this newfound utopia.

Holt

For the last two weeks, Izzy and I have alternated staying at her place and mine. It's been beyond perfect just being together, openly holding hands, stealing kisses wherever we feel the need. It's heaven like this, just being ourselves—just breathing Izzy.

Bryson's wedding is in a week, and Dad offers to take both my brother and me to lunch before shooting a bucket of balls at the local driving range.

Dad's deep summer tan glows off his salmon colored polo. He's put on a little weight since his own engagement, but he looks happy for the first time in a long while, and I guess, in the end, that's all that matters—sort of.

"You take the boat out lately?" Dad nods as if I've already said yes.

"I haven't taken it out in forever. Been meaning to, though." I think Izzy and I are in the right place. Can't wait to get her out on the water and wrap my arms around her as we cruise the Atlantic.

"If you ever want to get rid of it, I'll take it off your hands." He looks to my brother. "How about you? Looks like you're jumping into a whole new ocean yourself. You ready to be a husband and a father?" Dad lifts his glass to Bryson as if he were toasting the idea.

"Just a husband for now." Bry shoots me a look that says no way to the baby stroller just yet. "Baya has a few years left in school, and I want to get a little more established before heading to the nursery."

Dad shakes his head. "We make plans, and God laughs—the women in our lives laugh, too." A grin slicks across his face, easy as an I told you so. "You think you've got it all laid out, but I give it a year before you tell me I'll be a grandfather soon enough. Women are wily. Once they get their heart set on something, there's no letting go. Don't think for a minute you have any say in it. You'll be a father when she's good and ready. Usually sooner than later."

What's this woman are wily bullshit?

That night comes back to me. I still remember the way the air was scented thick with pines—the way it felt to stuff a hundred dollar bill in Mona Tristin's icy hand.

I shake myself free from the memory.

"Baya is different." Bryson leans back in his seat. Any joy he might have felt about this afternoon has been efficiently sucked out by our father. "She and I want the exact same things out of life, but if that were to happen— it'd be an accident, one that we'd work around together."

"Fifty bucks says you'll be working around an accident in about six months time." A laugh sputters from him as he slaps Bryson over the shoulder. "No worries, son. We all go through it. It's just a part of being a man. "How about you, Holty? You got a sexy little vixen tying you to a chair these days? Watch the boys." He points his fork toward his chinos before taking a bite of his veal. "It's the first thing they go for once they realize they've got you hogtied."

"The boys are safe. I assure you. And, yes, actually, there is someone I'm seeing." I shoot a quick glance to my brother, and he raises a brow. "We're sort of low key."

"You might remember her," Bryson offers. "Izzy Sawyer? Her mom owns that dance studio we used to take Annie to."

"Oh yeah—the mother with the crazy eyes and helmet hair. I just spoke with her at your engagement party. She used to scare the shit out of me, always ready with a zinger. Now that's the kind of woman who knows how to keep a man in line." He cracks an imaginary whip. "If her daughter is anything like that, I say run for the hills."

"Nope. She's an angel." For as much as Iz loves her mother, she's the furthest thing from her.

"She's about your age right? I remember her. Both girls had that same jet black hair as their mom."

"That's her sister, Laney," Bryson offers. "She's the one getting married to Ryder. Izzy's a little older."

"No shit." Dad looks over to me, amused. "Are we talking about the spinster?"

That's how Izzy's mother introduced her.

"That would be the one."

"How much older we talking—a year? Two?"

"Five." I shove a bite of tenderloin in my mouth because the age difference doesn't mean a damn thing to me.

"Five?" He tugs at his day-glow collar as if his food just went down the wrong pipe. "That's half a decade! She'll be thirty in like five minutes. Is that what you want? To be in your twenties, stuck hanging out with some thirty year old?"

"Yes." I take a swig of my beer. I'll need all the benefits this bottle can give me to survive the afternoon.

"I get it"—he saws through his steak—"you're having a good time. Enjoy it. The woman you're really meant to be with hasn't even hit junior high yet. And there's a lot to be said about dating an older woman at your age. They're experienced. I dated an older woman once, right before I met your mother. She taught me some of the best tricks I know." He shakes his head as if reliving the memory.

"I'm not in this for tricks. And I promise you the woman I'm meant to be with isn't in grade school. It's Izzy." I glance at my brother. "As sure as Bryson is about Baya—and you are about Jenny—I'm that much more positive about Iz." I threw in that part about him and Jenny more as a barb, but he's too egotistical to realize it.

"Jenny and me aren't happening." He taps his hand over the table and swallows hard. "She took off last week. Something to do with an old boyfriend. I knew it wouldn't last—most things don't."

I look to Bryson. It's not true, and we both know it. Life is what you make of it, and so are relationships.

"Maybe you just haven't found the right one, yet." Bryson nods into his moronic theory as if he were being sincere.

"Dude—Mom was the right one." I glance back at Dad. "You had a good thing until I screwed it up." I trap my next breath in my lungs because I had no intention on letting that slip.

"You mean *I* screwed it up," Dad corrects. "It's true, I did, but I don't think your mother and I were built to last. No offense to her. Great woman." He shakes his head with a wistful smile. "All I'm saying is that sometimes a relationship simply doesn't work out. It runs its course. It's the way of the world."

It runs its course? That's just bullshit people who have fucked up relationships use to comfort themselves. And, the way of the world? I'm pretty sure it's love that makes the world go around and not a series of serial breakups. Since when is he so jaded? Is this some aftereffect of what happened that night or has he always been this way?

"Have fun with your lady friend." He gives me a quick wink. "But don't forget to keep an eye out for someone who'll look good on your arm for the long haul. Anybody can be *nice*." He says nice as if it were a dirty word defined solely as a means of manipulation. "Trust me there are a lot of nice people in this world. Nice is a dime a dozen—but beauty—that can be a tough diamond to mine. In the business world, it's all about how gorgeous that woman by your side is. Those guys are the true winners in life. The one who scores the hottest piece of ass wins. Beauty trumps age." He stabs into his steak. "Don't forget who told you so. There's not one successful billionaire with an old hag hanging all over him. They're dating supermodels—women thirty and forty years their juniors." He takes an anxious bite of his food and swallows it down. "Youth is the name of the game, and if you don't have it, you buy it in the form of a beautiful girl."

"And then what?" Bryson folds his arms across his chest. He's had just about as much of my father's bullshit as I have. "You trade her in for a new model when she shows her first wrinkle?"

Dad jabs his fork in my brother's direction. "Now you're catching on."

Nice. My father is a moron, and it took twenty-two years for me to realize it. Better now than never.

We finish up lunch and head back to the Black Bear. Neither Bryson nor I are up for spending any more time with our father this afternoon.

Maybe ever.

ജഇ

The next night, Bryson and Baya have an informal party at the Black Bear with their friends and everyone even mildly associated with the double wedding. Cole and I plan on taking my brother and Ryder out for some surf and turf on Friday—maybe catch a flick after. I guess we've all crossed titty bars off our to-do list, and I don't feel bad about it. I don't need those kinds of places, those kinds of girls in my life, to make me feel like a man.

Izzy walks in sporting a tight black dress that ends mid-thigh and heels that elongate her legs to the stratosphere. Izzy is the only thing I need in my life to make me feel like a man.

I walk over and drop a kiss to her lips. "Hey, darlin,'" I whisper directly into her ear, and she shivers beneath me.

"Hey, cowboy." She digs her fingers into the back of my hair. "Looks like everyone's here."

"And then some. Annie's been amassing new friends by the minute, and each one of them showed tonight for free appetizers. Can I get you something?"

"I'm starved. You want to split some nachos?"

"Sounds good." I put in our order, and we take a seat next to Annie and her buddies.

"So"—one of Annie's friends pipes up while openly checking me out—"you're the available one, huh?" Her hair is up in two perfectly curled pigtails, making her look all of thirteen. She's grinning at me, ear to ear, running her tongue over her lips as if it was a racetrack, and I know where this is headed.

"Nope, not me." I try to scoot into Iz and wrap my arm around her, but the chairs are so wide they manage to keep us a good foot apart.

The girl leans into Izzy. "Can we trade seats?"

"No." Izzy glares at her for a second. She doesn't look amused by the fact this girl is trying to steamroll her. "We're sharing a meal." She blinks a smile. "And, if I'm way over there, he might leave hungry." She slits her a look that says back off, this boy is mine.

"Oh, I'll make sure that boy gets everything he needs." She skims her teeth over her lip as if she were getting ready to take a bite out of my balls.

"Excuse me?" Izzy scoots back. Her voice pitches enough to let everyone within earshot know she's pissed.

"No need to get touchy." The girl tugs at a pigtail. "It's just that I think your brother is hot. That's one of the things I promised myself I'd do when I got into college—spend way more time with hot boys." She raises her brows in my direction, and, holy shit, Iz looks like she's ready to rip her a new one. "You don't want to stand in the way of a young girl's ambitions, do you?"

"First, you can have all the ambitions your little girl self wants. And second, he's not my brother." Iz looks over at me, a smile playing on her lips. "He's my boyfriend."

The girl in the pigtails breaks out in a cackle. "Yeah, right." Annie nods, and she stops cold. "No shitting, huh?" She sinks in her seat a little. "I swear, I thought you were kidding. I mean—you're pretty and stuff, I just didn't think you were together. You're like older."

"Nice." Izzy forces a smile to come and go.

"To each his own, right?" She adds, further burying herself in the hole. "I mean it's not a big deal. Men do it all the time. I hope when I'm as old as you, I can do the same thing. You're an inspiration. I think we should toast." She and her friends are quick to pick up their glasses. "What's your name?"

Izzy seals her lips tight. Clearly she's not up for any of their sorority girl games.

"Okay, fine"—the girl smirks—"to the older woman sitting at our table. Thank you for blazing a trail for the future cougars of America." She laughs under her breath at the dig.

"To the future cougars of America!" Her friends chime in, and it's a bitch-fest all around.

"We'll be *manthers*." The girl next to her howls.

"We'll be the hottest MILFs around!" She hacks out a laugh as if she's already wasted.

Both Annie and her friend, Marley, look stunned as shit. It's nice Annie has at least one friend with her head screwed on straight.

I lean into Izzy and whisper, "Let's get out of here." The night has already turned into crap on toast.

"No. Tonight is a big deal to your brother—Laney, too. Really, I'm fine." The hard expression on her face says she's not, but who could blame her for being pissed? "We just need to get used to the fact that people can be dumbasses." Izzy says it while looking straight at the rude girls still nursing their drinks, and the smiles fade right off their faces.

A stunted silence crops up at our end of the table.

"We should never get used to bullshit." I lean in. "Come here." I touch my finger under her chin and pull her toward me until our lips find one another. There's not a whole lot our kisses can't cure.

The girls break out in a round of oohs and awws and one audible *eww*.

Crap.

Izzy gets up and excuses herself for a minute.

Izzy is right.

People can be dumbasses.

11

Love Like This

Izzy

Dear Dad,

Sometimes I wish I had tougher skin. You would think between you taking off and a mother who says it like it is, I'd have my heart wrapped in barbed wire but I don't. I'm open and exposed, all flesh, no bone. Words cut me deeper than knives, and I'm perfectly capable of bleeding out from the wounds.

Soft shelled in Hollow Brook,
~Iz

ಬಿ೦ಲ್ಠ

Cougar.

I make an excuse about the inability to control my bladder at my age and head to the bathroom, locking myself in the furthest stall possible—ironically the same stall Holt and I claimed for ourselves a few weeks back.

Who knew girls could act so ridiculous? *Me*, that's who. I should know—half the teenagers at the dance studio create enough drama to power a nuclear reactor.

The door to the restroom opens, and two sets of heels click their way in.

"Why would she just take off like that?" A familiar voice vents in frustration.

It's Laney.

I suck in a quick breath.

Great. Now I've ruined her party. My finger closes over the latch, and just as I'm about to open it, I hear her give an exasperated sigh.

"I mean, what did she *think* was going to happen?"

My heart sinks. This is Laney—my baby sister who I fought all those years to protect. Couldn't she do the same for me for all of five minutes?

"It's not that big a deal." I recognize Baya's voice. "She's a big girl, and he's a big boy. They both know it's going to be tough at times. It's a cruel world. You and I know that."

Tough at times?

"Tell me about it. After all that B.S. that my mother *and* Ryder's mom put us through—I know exactly how cruel it can be. And that was just from family. It's never easy. But, you know, this is different."

I try to even my breathing in an effort to hear them better.

"How so?" Baya asks the question for me. I'm starting to like her better by the minute. And why is Laney so narrow-minded all of a sudden?

"Izzy is—" she gives an exasperated sigh—"I don't know. She's just always been a little different."

What? I'm not different. Am I different?

"Well, not always"—Laney continues—"but for a while now." My stomach bites with heat because suddenly I know where this is going. "It's like the entire world has her paranoid. It's as if she's afraid to admit she's got some deep-seated psychological issues. She's been skittish around guys for as long as I can remember, so it doesn't surprise me she's not in a normal relationship."

Just wow.

I bust through the stall, and both Laney and Baya look as if they've seen a ghost.

"Excuse me." I huff an incredulous laugh. "But I'd hate to hide out in a bathroom stall and exhibit any more of my *deep-seated* psychosis."

"Izzy, I'm so sorry!" Laney steps into me, and tries to take hold of my arm, but I move out of the way. "Look, I didn't mean any of that."

"Yes, you did. You meant every word."

"For the record"—Baya raises her hands in the air as if this were a stick up—"I swear to you, I think what you and Holt have is totally fine. In fact, my mom will be in town in a few days, and I really think you should talk to her. She loved my father. She would be your biggest cheerleader."

"Yeah, well, too bad my sister won't be making the team." I speed toward the exit just as that sassy pigtail-wearing bitch from the table makes her way in, and I jam my shoulder into hers on the way out. I may or may not have meant to do that. I can't decide if it was a happy accident or if I finally grew some balls.

"Watch it!" Her friend barks in my direction.

"Never mind," Pigtails shouts. "She can't see well. She's old."

I can still hear their cackles as I dive into the crowd and try to lose myself in the congestion of bodies. The music is so loud my head pounds with its annoying hammer-like backbeat.

"Izzy." Laney pulls me in by the arm. "I swear to you, I'm *sorry*." Her features crumble as if she's about to cry. "I didn't mean any of it. It just bubbled out of me like verbal diarrhea. Please, can we just forget this ever happened?"

"No, because it *did* happen. And stop saying you didn't mean it." I bite the air with my words. "You were right. I *am* a freak. And you want to know why? Because I've been too busy protecting *you!* I wanted you to grow up without any of the bullshit I had to deal with. I wanted you to have a healthy, happy life. You're the reason I've stayed in that shit house all along. I didn't go to college, Laney, because I stayed home to watch out for you. So next time, instead of telling the world what a nutcase I am, how about just saying thank you!" I bolt deeper into the bar.

Okay, so I may have left my mother from of the equation temporarily as to why I've hung out at home for so long, but for the most part every word is true.

I thread through a thicket of bodies. I just want to find Holt and get the hell out of here. I want to head to his place and not come out for weeks.

An odd sight snags my eye. I spot Holt facing the other way while a tiny little hand slithers up and down his back.

What the?

A bleached barfly hacks out a laugh while her hands continue to ride up and down his body.

Shit.

He gingerly plucks her off, but it's too late, I'm too far gone. My sanity has already plunged off a cliff. I'm swan diving into the rocks below, and there's no parachute, no one around to stop me from what I'm about to do next.

"Izzy." He steps back, his face darkening as if he were embarrassed.

"No—I get it." I close my eyes for a moment. "You're attractive, and look at her—she's beautiful." I swallow hard while examining the bimbo who was molesting the hell out of my boyfriend a moment ago. *Boyfriend*. What a joke. "Laney was right. We're not normal." The girl backs away, and Laney and Baya take her place. I glance to Holt and his stunned expression. "There are tons of girls your age and *younger* who would die for a chance with you."

His features flex with a cloud of grief.

"*Iz*, I swear, she just sprung out from nowhere. I plucked her off as soon as I could." Holt wraps his arms around me, but I'm quick to push him away.

"Look"—I nod over at Jemma's sister, Marley—"there's someone who'd be perfect for you. She's nice, and I know she likes you."

"I'm not into her. I'm into you." Holt doesn't take his eyes off me. "What the hell happened?" He turns to Laney. "What the fuck did you say to her?"

Ryder and Bryson show up, ready for a fight.

"I have to get out of here." I slip out of Holt's grasp.

My phone goes off, and I fish it from my pocket. It's a group text from Mom to my sister and me.

FYI, your father just walked through the door.

"Oh my, God," I whisper, leaning against the wall to keep from passing out.

Laney and I head for the exit. She rides home with me, but we don't say a word.

Somehow we've both fallen through the rabbit hole tonight.

Things were getting pretty wild back there, and, now—dear God, my father is back.

But something tells me it won't be such a happy ending. Today has already been hit by a shit storm. After all, I've just lost the only other man that has ever meant anything to me.

I just lost Holt.

೮ೕഗ൭

Laney and I hit the driveway and storm into the house. There's no car out front. No news crews or crowd amassing at the door to document our miracle.

"*Mom*?" I shout, tearing through the empty living room and into the kitchen.

"Come here, girls." Mom stands with her face slicked with tears.

A tall, muscular man, older with a graying goatee stands alongside her. I recognize those navy eyes, that stern, lantern-jawed face.

"*Daddy*." I rush over and collapse my arms around his thick, solid waist. Here it is. I've finally lost my sanity and willed my father into being. Tears brim to the surface as I drown in a sea of unfathomable emotion.

Holt and Ryder burst into the room.

"Izzy?" Holt comes at me as if I might be in danger.

"I'm okay." I wipe down my face with the back of my hand. "This is my dad." I look up at him, this phantom, this ghost I've pulled from deep in my memory. "Since the minute he left, I never stopped believing he'd be back one day." I run my hands over his shirt just to feel how real he is—how believable my fantasy had become. He's older— with far more silver in his hair than the jet-black I remember. He looks hardened. His eyes say they've experienced two lifetimes worth of grief.

"Where were you? And why did it take so long for you to man up and come back?" I can hardly believe the words as they spill from my lips.

"Prison." He doesn't hesitate with the answer.

Ryder wraps his arms around Laney, and suddenly I want to do the same. It's always been Laney I've wanted to protect against the madmen my mother brought into the house. And now I wonder if the most deranged of them all was my father.

"Your dad never left us." Mom buries her face in her hands for a moment. "They took him away." She looks to my sister, her lips quivering out of control. I've never seen my mother so distraught, so fragile. "Sweetie, we didn't think he was coming back. Once they threw the book at him, we thought it best to just move on."

"What happened?" I'm not so sure I want to know, but we've come this far.

"Killed a man in a bar fight." He gives a weak smile that dissipates as quick as it came. "He was going after your mother, and I lost my cool. I cold-clocked him. He fell to the ground and never woke up."

Oh God. I shoot Mom a look. "Find a man who'll kill for you, and that's your pot of gold, huh?" I think I've demystified her macabre riddle. It takes all of my effort to restrain my anger for being lied to all these years. "It sounds to me like you omitted a few important details."

"I was never out to trick you." Mom wags her head with attitude. "I said he left, and he did. Your father and I decided it was best you not know. We didn't want you thinking he was a coldblooded killer because he's not. What happened was an accident. And, at the house, we never talked about it in depth. You never probed, Izzy—you never asked questions."

"That's because I didn't know what I needed to ask!" My voice reverberates over the small room. "Did you ever *ask* why the hell I was so afraid of every damn man you dragged into the house?"

She inches her head back as if she had just been slapped.

"That's right. Remember Chuck? I believe your cute little pet name for him was Chuck the Fuck? Well, guess what? He was trying to fuck more than just you."

"Shit!" My father thunders as he slaps his hand down onto the table, and now he looks as if he wants to kill my mother, too.

My body goes numb. My stomach turns into lava, and vomiting doesn't sound like such a bad idea.

Here my father is back, and, instead of appreciating the moment, instead of accepting it for what it was, I threw every form of misery I had ever encountered into my parent's faces.

"I'm sorry." I bolt out of the house, and Holt appears beside me on the porch.

"Come here." He wraps his arms around me, and I lose it. I bury my face in his warm, familiar chest and sob for what feels like weeks. It's safe like this with him. Holt is the only real and tangible thing in my life right now.

"I'm sorry." His voice cracks as he takes in a quick breath. "I'm so sorry about what happened to you." He presses his lips over my ear, panting into me with his grief. "Just say the word, and we can be anywhere."

"Little Bit?" My father's voice resonates from the living room as he makes his way over, and I melt straight down to my soul. "I've waited twenty long years to see your pretty face again." He chokes on his words. "I understand if you don't want to see me." He steps outside, wiping down his cheeks. "But I'd sure appreciate it if you'd stay a minute longer."

Here he is, alive and in the flesh. He's real, not some figment of my imagination. This is happening. It's no dream.

Holt and I head back into the house together. We sit for hours listening to my mother and father tell stories about the past, filling Laney in on a world she never knew.

My father thought they had locked him up and threw away the key. He and my mother were simply trying to protect us.

I take in the beautiful man by my side, and the beautiful man in front of me. I have two wonderful men in my life—Holt and my father, the only two men that I've ever really needed in order to breathe.

And here I am wondering if I should let either of them back into my world.

Holt

The night before the wedding, Cole and I take Ryder and Bryson out for their last meal as free men.

The Carving Board is a ritzy steakhouse that sells cow carcass for the price of gold per ounce.

"Where the hell do they get their cattle? Middle earth?" Cole nearly passes out as he scans the prices.

"Take it easy," Ryder says it calm while perusing the menu. "Tonight it's my treat."

"No it's mine," I offer. "You two are the ones putting your balls in a noose. It's the least I can do."

"Balls in a noose?" Bryson shakes his head. "Say one more boneheaded thing around Izzy, and you'll be begging her to noose your balls as she's walking out the door."

"What's that supposed to mean?"

"It means she's sensitive, in the event you haven't noticed. And I'd like to see you make things work, so put a muzzle on it."

"Got it." For once it seems he's right. "We've spent the last few days and nights together, and she still hasn't opened up to me about what happened." I guess I got the rough and dirty side of it. I thought she might want to have a private conversation about it. I don't need a lot of details. I just thought we should at least try to process it together.

Ryder tips his beer in my direction. "Laney said his name was Chuck Dupree. Said he was a crazy fucker who drank the day away while their mother slaved at the studio."

Chuck Dupree. I tuck the name away for later.

"So tomorrow is the big day, huh?" I change the subject. I'm in no mood to share my thoughts on what I'd like to do to Chuck the Fuck. Things are going to get fucked all right. He single handedly destroyed the woman I love, and I plan on returning the favor—after the wedding of course. No use in screwing up the wedding day photo-shoot with a black eye in the event Chucky plans on fighting back.

"Big day is right." Cole slaps Bryson over the shoulder. "We've come a long way from the scoreboard era."

"Damn straight." Bryson knocks back half his beer.

Bryson and Cole once had an infamous monument to the chicks they bagged, etching them on the wall by way of tally marks. But Baya and Roxy cured them of that. Laney cured Ryder of walking around like he was a big shot, even though he sort of was one. And Izzy, well, I do believe she cured me of not believing in fairytales. I think I might deserve someone—might even deserve a happily ever after with Snow White herself.

Bryson knocks me in the shoulder. "What's the goofy grin for?"

"I think I'm finally settling into the idea of being with someone. I feel empty without Izzy, and the thought of doing this life thing without her makes me sick to my stomach. She's the one—and I'm damn glad about it."

Bryson lifts his beer, and everyone at the table does the same.

"To finding the one. By some miracle we all seemed to find her."

"To the one." We toast and spend the rest of the night laughing our asses off at the stupid fucks we used to be.

The girls made us better people.

Something tells me they always will.

⁝⁞

Saturday, the sun is bright, the weather a toasty seventy-nine degrees as we stand in the perfectly manicured yard of Ryder's parent's estate. Miles of white lawn chairs are laid out in rows, and every single one is filled to capacity. I'd bet the Black Bear that all of Whitney Briggs showed up for the big event.

The gazebo is decked out with enough white roses to outfit every prom in a sixty-mile radius. It looks beautiful, elegant, and I'll be damned if it doesn't bring a tear to my eye. I take in a hard sniff, trying to avoid the boo-hoo fest welling up in my chest.

Bryson and Ryder stand at the base of the gazebo, with me next to my brother.

My father and mother sit side by side down front, and my heart breaks for them but not in the traditional way it usually does when I see them together. This time there's a genuine grief that has very little to do with what happened that day back in high school. A thought comes to me, and I hold my breath a moment. This is a day of new beginnings, of fresh starts. For a second I toy with the idea of letting everyone in on my dirty secret—but then the memory of Mom's face, the horrible cry that escaped her throat that day comes back to me. Who the hell was I to rip open old wounds? To pour battery acid in them for the hell of it just to try and make myself feel better. Nope not going there. My stomach twists in knots.

A stringed quartet starts in on a beautiful piece. It sounds like a dove crying out to God. Izzy appears like a dream, like a tall glass of water in a vast dusty land, and the sky gets a little brighter.

"God almighty," I whisper.

"Keep it in your pants," Bryson mumbles. "It's my lucky day, remember?"

Tears blur my vision as she glides her way over. Her hair is swept to the side. Her eyes blaze like fire. As far as I'm concerned, Izzy has already outshined the brides. Heaven help me. I think Bryson has it wrong. I think it's my lucky day. Hell, every day with Izzy in it is my lucky day.

Roxy and Annie head down next. I can't get over how grown up Annie looks. It gets me that much closer to tears. The music switches to the all-familiar bridal march.

Bryson takes one look at Baya and loses it. Cole walks his sister down the aisle, and it's an emotional scene, not a dry eye in the house, not even mine. I know they lost their dad a while back, and seeing Cole step up to the plate has me wanting to boo hoo with the best of them.

Ryder lets out an audible breath, waiting for his own bride to make her way to him.

Laney appears, beautiful in her own right. She walks down with her mother on one side and her father on the other. For a moment, I imagine it's Izzy, and a lump the size of a fist gets trapped in my throat. By the time the girls are at their sides, both Ryder and my brother have rivers slicking down their cheeks. The ceremony goes off without a hitch. No one passes out from the heat. No one objects to the state of the unions. And, before I know it, the boy I grew up with both in and out of utero is a bona fide married man. The brides and grooms take off running down the aisle as the crowd breaks out in a celebratory applause. I hook my arm in Izzy's and pause as we make our way under the arch.

"You mind if I steal a kiss?"

Izzy sheds a mile-wide smile. "I'd be upset if you didn't."

I lean in and plant a sweet kiss right over her lips, and, for a brief moment, I imagine this is our wedding day. It feels like magic. Like something I've secretly waited my whole life to do with Izzy. I know I've wanted it. And now it's right here in our grasp.

The reception takes place right after the ceremony. Rue Capwell has this place operating like a five-star restaurant with enough food to feed a football stadium. After dinner, a live band starts up, and the crowd mixes both on and off the dance floor.

Izzy sways in my arms as we stand just beyond the masses. I warm her back with my hands, brushing a gentle kiss over her ear.

"You want to dance?" I rock our bodies to set the mood.

"I was thinking we could take a little walk." Her eyes widen, pale and round as the full moon above. "This place is huge. Rumor has it there's a pond out there somewhere."

"Sounds like we should find it."

I snap up two champagne glasses from the roving waiters, and we begin to make our way outside the crowd.

"Well, look who's here!" Laney waves us over to herself and Ryder. "You're not leaving are you?"

"Nope." Izzy offers her sister a quick embrace. "We thought we'd ditch the crowd for a moment."

"Okay, but find me before all this madness ends." She bears into her sister. "And as soon as I get back from my honeymoon I want to get together. I want us to talk about things the way we used to. I want to know you and everything you're willing to share with me because I love you, Iz."

Izzy swallows hard. "Done. You're on for coffee when you get back."

"Coffee." She holds up a finger as she and Ryder fade into the crowd.

I hand Izzy a glass of champagne and wrap an arm around her waist.

"Do you think you're ready to talk about things with me?" I trace my lips over hers. If she doesn't want to, I'm not pushing it ever again. "I'd love for you to open up, but only if you're ready."

"Yeah, I think it's time." She pulls back and inspects me under the moonlight. "Holt—is there something you've been holding back from me?" She cuts me a look that says she wants answers. "Because if there is, I'd like for you to open up as well."

I knock back the champagne.

I plan on telling Izzy everything—right now.

12

The Whole Story

Izzy

Dear Dad,

I guess I don't really have to write you these letters anymore since you've come back, but old habits die hard. I'm so glad you're in our lives again. I feel full now. Does that make sense? Between you and Holt it feels as if my cup is running over.

I love you so much.
~Izzy

෨෬

When Laney was seven years old, the exact age I was when our father mysteriously vanished from our lives, she put on a white dress and declared herself a bride. She said she was going to marry a prince and live in a castle—be a princess forever. I'd say she's batting a thousand. I guess she knew what she was talking about after all.

Laney was always the kind of girl who knew what she wanted and went after it. She had goals, ambitions, and, most importantly, standards regarding who she would and wouldn't allow into her life. God knows she didn't get that from my mother.

"What's going through your mind?" Holt pulls my hand to his lips and peppers it with kisses.

"Laney once said she'd marry a prince and live in a castle." A dull laugh trembles through me. In truth, I'm giddy for my sister beyond belief. Today may have been her wedding day, but it's also the day I pass the baton to Ryder. I know he'll always keep her safe, perhaps a little better than I ever could.

"If it means anything, Ryder lives in some fancy high-rise, so I guess that qualifies as a castle."

"That's good enough for me. It's been my dream to see her ride off into the sunset—in a good way."

"I know what you mean. I'm happy for Bryson, too." He leads us under a willow, and then we see it.

The moon pours its reflection over a black pool of water, smooth and glassy, like a giant mirror shinning into the night.

"Looks like we found the pond." He buries a kiss in my neck.

"More like a lake." It's huge with the borders stretching out far into the night.

"Check this out." Holt plucks a metal pontoon from a nearby bush and pushes it towards shore. "You think we should take this for a spin?"

"Sounds like a dream."

Holt helps me into the tiny boat and jumps on board just as we sail from shore. He pulls an oar off the floor and rows us toward a marshy swamp where the reeds grow six feet above the waterline.

"You ready to do this?" He shakes out the oar and carefully places it by our side.

"Your secret or mine," I blow it out in a whisper. "How do we decide who goes first? Rock-paper-scissors?"

"I couldn't think of a more democratic way."

We shake our fists at each other while chanting, rock—papers—scissors, in unison. The sound of our joy—our laughter, echoes up to the dusty lavender sky. There's not a star in heaven that didn't show up for this event tonight.

"Paper covers rock. You win," I say. "So I guess I go first." I glance down and play with the ribbon wrapped around my waist.

Holt slides over and pulls me into his lap. He lands his lips to my cheek and holds them there a good long while.

"You don't have to do this."

"I do," I say it so fast I'm half afraid I'll blurt the truth out before I've had the chance to formulate the proper words. "Okay, here it goes." I take a breath and close my eyes. That day floods back like the nightmare it was. The memories suck me in like a tornado. It carries me high in its dark dizzying funnel, threatening to drop me back to earth and watch me shatter all over again. "When my father left, it was a scary time for me. Laney was too young to realize it, so things were a little different for her. Anyway, right afterwards, we moved and my mother purchased the studio. She ended up spending a fair amount of time there. Usually when she worked, she'd leave us girls home with whoever was her main squeeze at the moment." A tear rolls down my cheek, and I wipe it away. "My mother, being her overbearing self, had a way of attracting the lowest of the low. But, for some reason, I liked the thought of having a man around almost as much as she did. I wanted someone—anyone to come in and try to take my daddy's place. Deep down I knew they couldn't but that didn't stop me from holding out for a miracle. Anyway, by the time I was thirteen the new string of wannabe daddies started to pay me a little too much attention if you know what I mean. They were interested in more than just reading me a bedtime story. Suddenly there were grabby hands and lips that found their way far too close to mine. One day, Laney walked in the room and one of them started to lay his hands on her, so I became a barrier. I made sure she was safe and they wouldn't think of touching her. Of course, I told my mother, but they always denied it, and she always believed them. So I did what I had to—I ran them all out." My body goes numb. A breeze comes up, and the tears drip down my cheeks in an icy luge. "I beat them. I threatened them with fake video footage that I would take to the police if they didn't leave overnight, and they almost always did. Some were tougher to get rid of than others. One of them told me that I was a nasty little bitch and would get mine one day."

Holt tightens his grip over me. "Fucking pieces of shit."

"You got that right. But I had made a promise to my dad the day he said goodbye that I'd make sure my mother was never alone, and that's what I intended to do—be right there with her." I blow out a breath. "So here's the big one." My body trembles as the words jerk up my throat. I swore to myself that Jemma would be the last person I ever told. I guess I could break a promise to myself. This probably wasn't a healthy one to keep to begin with. "On the night before my eighteen birthday—it was almost the end of my senior year, and I had already been accepted to three different colleges—I was working a shift over at the studio." I twist into him and catch his gorgeous face as the moonlight kisses it with its translucent beams. "You were there."

"Me?" His eyes round out like twin globes.

"Yes, you." I sneak a kiss onto his mouth. "You came to pick up Annie with your mom, and for whatever reason you lingered in the studio. It was just the two of us. The music had just finished, and I was cleaning up—you looked right at me and said—"

"Izzy Sawyer you are the most beautiful creature I have ever seen," he finishes the sentence for me.

"You remember?"

"Heck, yes, I remember. It took me weeks to work up the courage to do that."

"*Holt.*" My chest heaves, and I try to restrain myself from bawling. "That was the last good moment. The last innocent part of who I was." I give a hard sniff. "I drove home. Mom had to take Laney to a friend's house, and she ended up staying, too. It was just me and Chuck. I could tell he'd been drinking, and I tried to go straight to my room, but he tackled me. No warning. No come here sweetie, why don't you sit by me for a while like he used to when he tried feeling me up. This was an all out assault. He jumped me right there on the living room floor, and, before I knew it, he was tearing off my clothes. I still had my leotard on and my dance tights, so it was near impossible for him to do anything but twist me up in a knot." I close my eyes. "I can still feel his hands on my body, squeezing my breasts until I thought I would burst. His fingers slithered south, and he did things I don't want to remember." I look up at Holt as tears roll down his face. "Um, he didn't, you know, but he came close. I was still a virgin when we—"

Holt lands his lips over mine to quell me, and I swallow down the rest of the words. Holt knows. A weight has been lifted off my body. An entire iron pot I've been carrying around with me all these years has slipped from my grasp, and I'm light as a feather. I'm finally set loose from the nylon chains I was fettered in all those years ago. Just speaking it out loud, right here to the man I love, set me free from the power that monster had over me all this time.

"As strange as it sounds, that felt good to get out," I whisper the words with a thread of shame.

"That doesn't sound strange at all. Izzy"—he blows a breath into my hair, warming me—"I want to find him and kill him."

"No. It's over. I'm fine, and Laney is fine. He took off the next day, and it was back to square one with Mom and her steady string of morons. None were ever as bad as he was. I was able to protect Laney until she was off to college. I hung around and made sure there were no more perverts—which there were, but I ran them all off, one by one. Also, I was determined to keep my promise to my father and not leave my mother alone. It was sort of my fault she was alone to begin with, but I couldn't let those assholes stay—and I knew if they couldn't I'd have to. It was a small price to pay."

"They were never going to stick around and be loyal to your mom, Iz. You did the right thing by kicking their asses out the door. She was sucking off the bottom of the pond, to put it mildly."

"I can see that now. And, with my dad back, it sort of eases the burden off me a bit."

"Are they together?"

"I don't know. He's staying at the house, but he's in Laney's old room."

"I guess it's all going to work out like it's supposed to."

"For the first time in a long time, I'm okay with that." A dull laugh rattles from my chest. "When I was a kid, before my dad left, I had this jar that I used to whisper my wishes and dreams into. It sounds insane, I know, but I thought that way I could always have them. I thought maybe someday when I was older I'd unleash them into the world, and they'd come true." I turn to face him fully and gaze up at his sharp cut cheeks, the brows that fan over his stainless-colored eyes. "And here you are. Every wish and dream I've ever had—alive and in the flesh."

His eyes shine like shards of broken glass. "Izzy"—he presses it out like a dying breath—"I want you to have that again. I want you to believe in all of your wishes and dreams. I want to be able to give you that."

"You already have." I press my lips to his, and neither of us moves, neither of us breathes. I pull back and take him in under the blanched light of the moon. "Holt Edwards, you are a masterpiece. You are one of the most beautiful creatures I have ever seen."

"I think you're pretty damn amazing, Iz. You're the only gorgeous creature I see. And I love that you were storing up all of your wishes and dreams for someday." He brushes the hair from my face. "I'm glad I'm part of that." He drops a kiss onto my lips once again and lingers. "My turn, huh?"

"If you're ready."

"I am. I hope." Holt starts in on a heartbreaking story I never expected to hear, and my insides wrack with grief for him.

Holt doesn't think he deserves to be with anyone, ever. It's like we're the very same person. Can two people like us ever make things work?

I hope this confessional didn't just damn our relationship to hell.

And a small part of me thinks it may have.

But both Holt and I have already been to hell and back—I don't see why we couldn't withstand one more trip together.

Holt

Two weeks later

For so long I held things close to the vest, so when it finally came time to open up it was like cutting myself loose from an anchor. I could see the light above on the surface—I knew there was good, clean air to fill my lungs with up there, and, as soon as I spoke the words to Izzy, I could feel myself corking to the top—breathing once again without anything weighing me down. After Izzy let her demons fly, I knew I could, too. We sat in that tin boat for hours after that just holding each other tight. It was a night I'd like to both remember and forget. It carved itself over our hearts, and the wounds sizzled as we poured out our grief. But, over the last two weeks, Izzy and I have been soaring higher than ever. I never thought I could feel so close to someone, still not sure I deserve to. That's why Izzy is coming with me tonight to my mother's house where I've called a family meeting. Bryson is home from his honeymoon, so I asked if he could drop by, too.

"Looks like they're all here." I say as we head on in.

"There's Annie." Izzy nods to my sister on the porch swing.

"Hey, girl. Whatcha' doing out here?"

Look who I found, she signs with one hand while holding a white ball of fluff in the other. It's the tiniest kitten I've ever seen—nothing but fur and bright blue eyes.

"Oh my, gosh!" Izzy lunges at the poor fuzz ball until Annie surrenders it. "Where did you ever find this gorgeous creature?"

Out back. Mom says I can't keep him.

"She says she found him out back. My mom is allergic to cats, so she has to find him a new home."

"Done," Izzy says it so fast my head spins.

"Whoa, what if I wanted him?" I give a cocky grin.

"Well, if you do, then we'll just have to share custody." The whites of her eyes shine in the night as she gives a tiny smile.

"I guess we'll just have to do that whole, Monday, Tuesday, Wednesday—Thursday, Friday thing."

"What about the weekends?"

"We'll just have to work things out." I drop a hot kiss over her lips, and the kitten purrs between us. "Or you could move in and save us both the hassle."

Izzy gasps. The porch light frames her in from behind and makes her glow like an otherworldly being, like an angel.

Hello, Annie signs. *I'm still here*. She taps Izzy on the shoulder. *And I think you should say yes. I still think you make a really cute couple.*

"She says you have to, or she'll hunt you down and kill you."

Annie kicks me in the shin.

"All right, she thinks you should say yes." I pull Izzy in until our stomachs touch. "She thinks we make a really cute couple."

Izzy presses her lips together and nods. She never takes those quicksilver eyes off mine. My chest floods with relief. My dick perks to life just looking at her, and suddenly I wish we were anywhere but standing on my mother's porch.

"You ready to do this?" She nods toward the house.

"I'm ready." I give the beast a gentle scratch between the ears. "So what should we name the cat?"

"How about *Happy*?"

"Happy." I let it settle in. "It's perfect." Happy is exactly the place I'm at these days.

We head inside with Annie and our new cat, Happy.

"Big bro." Bryson socks me in the arm before yanking me into a half hug. He pulls Izzy into a quick embrace as well.

"Izzy!" Baya hops over.

Bryson and Baya are both as pale as the day they left, an anomaly after spending a solid week in the Caribbean. They went with Laney and Ryder. Rumor has it they only saw each other once, and that was at the airport for the flight home. Not that I could blame them. I don't think I'd see much of the Caribbean either if Izzy and I were on our honeymoon.

"What's going on?" Dad comes over to where we're standing with Mom right on his heels.

"Let's take a seat." God knows we're going to need it. We head to the sofas, and I pull Izzy in close. I don't think I could have ever done this without her. Hell, I know I couldn't.

Annie catches my eye. She's so young. There's no way I want her to hear any of this bullshit.

"Annie"—I start—"I'm not sure you should be here for this."

Annie shoots Mom a knowing look before signing. *I'm plenty old enough. I'm part of this family. I have a right to be here. Besides, I've already moved into my dorm. I'm not a baby.*

"Fair enough." I take one final look around the room at the lives I managed to screw up on a dime all due to some stupid bet I made back in high school. "I apologize to each of you in advance. I never in my wildest dreams would have imagined that something I did on a whim all those years ago would land us where we are today."

"And where's that?" Mom tilts toward me, curious as to where I'm going with this.

"Here." I shoot a look to dad. "With you two divorced."

"What?" Bryson leans in. "Dude, let's go in the other room. Why don't you run this past me first? I can help you with whatever it is you're trying to do."

"No, trust me. It's better to just get this over with." I tighten my grip around Izzy's waist. "When I was in high school"—I look to my parents—"there was a weekend when I thought the two of you were away. Bryson and I were just hanging out here at the house, Annie was at a friend's." I swallow hard. "I thought"—tears come, and I'm quick to blink them away—"I thought Bryson was in the house. I went out to a movie with a bunch of people, and we all came back here. We were sitting on the porch, and I gave a hundred bucks to some girl that was with us and told her to go in and try to get my brother to sleep with her. We were all stoned out of our minds. It was stupid. *I* was stupid."

"I don't remember this." Bryson shakes his head at me a second too long as if telling me to knock this shit off.

"That's because—it turns out you weren't here either. You took off with your buddies. It wasn't you in the house."

"Oh my, God." Mom drops her face in her hands. "I remember that night."

"The Master's presentation?" Dad looks to Mom.

"Yes." She looks to Bryson and Annie. "Your dad and I were invited to speak at an entrepreneurship program upstate. At the last minute, it was canceled." Mom turns to me and shakes her head. "Honey, please, there's so much more to that story. I don't want you blaming yourself for something that was never your fault."

"What's the whole story?" Bryson is pissed and rightly so.

"I thought it was you, dude." My voice cracks as I say it. I knew you wouldn't go for her. I thought it was funny—one big joke." I come to a stop because I hate where this goes next.

"You can do it." Izzy blows the words in my ear along with a kiss.

"Okay. So the girl goes into the house, and about a half hour later Mom comes home and surprises the shit out of me. She heads inside, and I follow. The next thing I know, I hear screaming coming from upstairs. I run up to find Dad half dressed—Mom pissed as hell—and the girl I paid to hit on Bryson staggering out of the room, naked, with her clothes in her arms."

The room stills. It's all eyes on me. Maybe I should have put more thought into what I was going to say next.

"That's it, and I'm sorry."

"That's not it." Mom comes over and sits beside me. She wraps an arm around my shoulder and pulls me in. "You're blaming yourself for something that isn't your fault, Holt."

"It is my fault. I paid her to go upstairs and do what she did."

"I'm to blame." Dad pipes up. He groans, massaging his temples. "Is that why you didn't go to college?"

I don't say anything, just take a deep breath instead.

"Holt, you're bright," Dad starts. "Imaginative— sometimes too much so. But if you've been beating yourself up over that for all these years, you're also too damn hard on yourself."

"I'm the one that blew this family apart," I shout it a little louder than intended. Why the fuck can't they see I'm the one to blame?

"*I'm* the one that blew this family apart." Dad's face turns red with rage. "I'm sorry. I apologize to each and every one of you. But *I* did this, Holt. Not you. If it makes you feel better, it wasn't the first time I was unfaithful to your mother."

"It was the last straw, and so I kicked him out." Mom shrugs as if she's indifferent to it now. "It's over, Holt. It was over for me that weekend." She pulls me into a tight embrace. "Oh, honey. It kills me to think you've suffered with this all these years."

Bryson blows out a breath. "So why are you coming clean, now?"

"Izzy had to deal with her past recently, and I thought it best I do the same."

Annie gives a brief wave to get my attention. *I think you're brave to have told us these things. Nobody wants you to walk around with that kind of weight on your shoulders. But I'm shocked you would take the blame for it. Didn't it ever occur to you that it was Dad who made the final decision?*

"I know. I know Dad had the final say." I give Izzy's hand a squeeze. "But, when push came to shove, I thought—" Crap. I didn't know he had done it before. That might have changed the last few years of my life, but, in hindsight, I think I ended up right where I needed to be.

"You didn't blow this family apart, Holt." Dad comes over, and I stand as he slings his arm over my shoulder. "It was all my fault. I apologize for being anything less than the father you kids deserved. Could you find it in your heart to forgive me?"

"Always." I pull him in and let the tears fall onto his shoulder. A weight had been lifted, like a tractor rolling off my chest, I can finally breathe again. I pull back and take him and my mother in. "I know you don't want me to blame myself, but a part of me always will at least a little. You said so yourself, Mom, that it was the last straw."

"There was already someone else," Dad assures. "Believe it or not, I think you saved your mother from a lot more grief. It was best we parted ways when we did."

Mom clasps his shoulder until we're standing in a huddle. "Your father and I have always maintained an amicable relationship. At first, it was for the sake of you kids, but, now, it's because we're friends, and we always will be." She pulls my head up gently by the chin. "You're my son, and I love you. You did nothing malicious. You didn't mean to hurt anybody. Please, Holt, forgive yourself. As far as I'm concerned there's nothing to forgive."

"I feel the same." Dad touches his head to mine. "Let go of this. It's my burden, not yours. You were never meant to carry this."

Mom breaks out in a series of sneezes.

"I'd better get this little guy out onto the porch." Izzy cradles the tiny creature in her arms.

"I'll go with you," Baya says, and Annie follows along.

Bryson steps up and slaps me over the shoulder. "Wish you would have said something. I knew there was something eating at you. I just assumed it was the fact you didn't go to Briggs. You think you'll go now?"

"I'm good with the bars."

"Speaking of which." Bryson turns to Dad. "We got approved for the loan. Holt and I can buy you out at the asking price."

Dad lifts his brows, mildly amused. "How the hell'd you pull that off?"

"Got an outside investor to act as a silent partner." He looks to me. "If it's okay with you, Ryder says he'll spot us the loan."

"Ryder? That's great." I glance back to where Izzy was a second ago. Maybe I can get Laney and Ryder to spot the studio a loan as well? I know Izzy would die to have it.

We say goodnight, and Izzy and I hit the dark inky road with our new cat, Happy.

"You want to run by my place for while?"

"You mean our place?" Izzy's eyes light up with a smile born of a thousand promises, and my dick perks to attention.

"That would be the one." I steal a kiss as we drive off into the night.

A part of me is still convinced that things would have been a little different if I never started that tragic chain of events so long ago. But, in this case, I guess different doesn't mean better.

The past no longer has a hold of Izzy and me.

We're finally free, and we're going home—together.

But there are still a couple of things I need to do before we start in on that happily ever after.

13

Letters and Thank You Notes

Izzy

Okay Dad—here we go, last one.

They say all good things must come to an end. I'm not sure I necessarily believe that, but, in this case, I think that might be true. I think it's high time we start having real conversations with one another. I think it's high time we share more than ink and paper together. I'd like to see us move our relationship into the verbal zone. Now that I've had time to consider it, asking me to write to you proved to be a brilliant move. In a strange way it's as if you never left. I've always felt connected to you. I longed to sit down and write you each and every day. It was our special time. It was a season that I will cherish in and of itself because these letters that I thought were tiny tokens of my affection proved to be gifts to me, far more than you'll ever know.

Thank you for that. Thank you for being in my life every single day whether in body or spirit.

I love you more than words can say. So glad I can tell you in person.

Thank you for coming back to us.

Signing off for the very last time,
~Little Bit, all grown up.

ಐಲ್ಬ

Sunday afternoon, Mom, Laney, and I order take-out and talk to the man we never thought we'd see again, my father.

"I hope you like the lemonade!" Laney pours us each a glass. "It's my own recipe."

Mom rolls her eyes. "Hon, there are only three ingredients in lemonade, but we appreciate the effort." She takes a sip and makes a face. "Holy crap. You're lucky Ryder's pockets are lined with gold. This tastes like leprechaun piss."

"Nice, mother." Laney averts her eyes before taking a seat across from me.

Dad picks up Laney's hand, then mine. "You raised two beautiful girls here, Momma. I'm proud of each one of you."

"She did it all with the help of the studio." I look to Mom and nod. She has to know how much it means to me—to all of us.

Laney clears her throat and nods toward Dad. "So what's next for the two of you?" She means relationship wise, but she was nice enough to give them the out if they needed it.

Mom takes in a breath expanding the girth of her chest until her cleavage quivers.

"We're taking things slow," she whispers. "A lot of years have rolled under the bridge. We'll see if he can handle a woman like me."

Dad lets out a deep-throated laugh and warms me to the bone because it's the same laugh I remember from so long ago.

"I think I can take ya." He winks at her. "The truth is"—he looks to Laney and me—"I made it clear to your mom before I went in that she was free. We filed for divorce as soon as they threw away the key. I didn't think I'd ever get out, and I sure as heck didn't want her to suffer because of my sins."

"That man who died"—Laney says it just above a whisper—"did he have a family?"

"Mother, father"—dad blows out a breath—"no wife, two kids that were each with their own momma's. He was a drifter. Your mom and I went out for a night on the town, and he decided she would look real good sitting on his lap, so he tried to make it happen. I stopped him with a sucker punch, and the rest was history."

"His father hired an attorney that made sure your father fried." Mom claps her hands together once. "And, thankfully, he was paroled."

277

"What did you do before that?" Laney pulls her shoulders to her ears. "I mean, I don't really know that much about you. We heard you took off—end of story."

"I used to work the rail lines. I ran freight back and forth to the south. It kept me away a couple days a week, but it made coming home that much sweeter."

"I remember the day you left." Tears pool in my eyes. "You asked me to make sure Mom was never alone—to protect my little sister." I nod. "And to write."

His lips twitch somewhere between a smile and a good cry.

"Hang on—there's something I'd like to give you." I head to my room and speed back with the letters in hand. I hold them out as if I were offering a gift to the king, and in a way I am. My father was always my king, and our home was his castle. "I wrote you, Daddy." I hand over the impossibly huge stack of letters, all of them bundled in colorful rubber bands according to year. "I wrote you every day. It felt good to do this. I felt like you were still here, somehow—that I was talking right to you. Do you remember what else you said to me that day?"

A river of tears slick down my father's face as he quietly shakes his head.

A stone settles in my throat, but I push the words out anyway. "You said that you'd never be able to read them."

He cracks a smile—a ray of light that pierces right into my soul and fills in the darkness. "Honey, I love it when I'm wrong."

We share a soft laugh, as he pulls the wrapped bundles to his chest like a prize.

Mom's phone rings, and she stares at the screen a moment. "I think I need to take this." She picks up and starts in on a brief conversation that has her saying *okay*, and *that's great*, over and over. Mom ends the call and picks up her lemonade. "It was the realtor. Great news! I have a buyer for the studio." She cuts a look to Laney and me as her smile turns into a scowl. You could slice the air with my mother's displeasure over the fact we're not sharing in her elation. "Knock it off girls, this isn't the time. Pick up your damn glasses," she barks out the command. "To new beginnings."

We reluctantly lift our lemonade. "To new beginnings."

I take a quick sip.

Yup—leprechaun piss. That about sums up how I feel about losing the studio, too.

It feels like I'm losing my best friend, my invisible third parent. I guess when the universe gave me back my father, it needed to take one good thing away in order to make that happen. In a perfect world, I'd have both. But I'm glad my father is the last man standing.

I can't help think how perfect my life would be with both my father and the studio in it.

I guess I'll never know.

That night, much to my mother's horror, Holt helps me move three duffle bags filled with my stuff into his truck. Mom and Dad wave us off as we drive to Holt's apartment—my new home.

We park and head on up. Holt places my bags down just inside his door.

"You ready to do this, kitten?" He gives that cocky grin that I'm positive he invented just to make my insides melt.

"Only if you are."

He scoops me into his arms, and I let out a little scream mixed with laughter.

"I want to do this right." He carries me over the threshold and lands us softly onto the couch. "I think we should do a lot of things right." He tucks a kiss up by my ear. "I'm in this for the long haul, Izzy."

"Me, too, Holt." I dig my fingers into the back of his cool, soft hair. "I think there are a few fury people we forgot to bring."

He sucks in a quick breath. "Sounds like we need to make another trip." He starts to get up, and I pull him down by the shirt.

"Tomorrow." I give a quick wink. "We'll let grandma babysit just one more time."

A muted laugh drums from his chest. "That makes this the last night we get the whole place to ourselves."

I give a silent nod. "We should probably make the best of it."

"I'll make sure we will." Holt presses a soft kiss over my lips. "Thank you."

"For what?"

"For just being you."

His hands run up my thighs in one smooth motion as his heated skin connects with mine. Holt teases me with soft kisses as he lifts off my dress. He pulls back and examines me with my lace panties, my matching bra that I picked out just for him.

"Work of art," he whispers straight into my mouth. "Izzy Sawyer, you're the most beautiful creature I have ever seen."

"Thank you. I guess I should have said that a long time ago." My cheeks flood with heat. "There's one more thing I have to tell you." My throat runs dry at the thought of what's about to sail from my lips. I never thought I'd say these words. I never thought I'd want to. "I love you, Holt Edwards." I steady my eyes over his. "I'm madly, deeply, so far gone in love with you. I can't imagine my life without you in it."

Holt smiles at me with those luminescent eyes as if a lightning bolt were trapped in each one, unquenchable, unable to extinguish themselves if they tried.

"I love you, Izzy Sawyer." His expression grows serious. "And I didn't think I'd ever say those words up until you came into my life this summer. But the truth is, I loved you the first day I laid eyes on you. You've always held a place in my heart, Izzy. And you always will." His lips trail down my neck, straight down my chest through to my hip. Holt slides my panties off before lifting my knee and kissing the tip. He runs a long fiery kiss up through my thigh, to that tender part of me where he lingers. He moves up to my belly before raking his lips across my flesh all the way to my mouth. I greet him with my tongue, pulling him in by the hair as his body adheres to mine.

Holt makes love to me right there on the sofa. On the table, the floor, the bathroom before landing us on his ultra soft bed.

"Is this the grand finale?" I tease pulling the sheets up over us.

"More like the grand beginning."

Now this is a new beginning I can wrap my head around.

Holt dips his knee between my thighs and settles himself over my body. He pushes in nice and slow, diving onto my lips with a kiss that says welcome home, Izzy, and I love you all at once.

We're free at last.

Together forever.

This is our happily ever after—a brilliant beginning.

Holt

Laney and Ryder invite us over to their place for dinner. I met with them earlier in the week, and they both loved the idea of helping Izzy keep the studio. Tonight is the big reveal. After that, Ryder and I are going to take a little drive. I asked him to get as much info out of Laney about the dirtbag that touched Izzy when she was kid. He mentioned over the phone he knows where to find him—that we could go tonight if I wanted. Of course, I'm not saying a word to Iz. I'm pretty sure she'd try to stop me.

We ride up in the elevator and head toward the penthouse. It's fancier than hell, and, for a moment, I feel bad I can't give Izzy something this nice at this stage of our lives—hell, probably at any stage of our lives.

"I know what you're thinking." She traces her finger up my chest to my chin and makes me look at her. "As long as you're in my bed, we're in the right place."

"Music to my poor bartender ears."

"You're the new owner." She gives my sides a pinch. "Let's turn that whiskey into gold."

"With you by my side, that's exactly what I plan on doing."

Laney greets us at the door, and we sit down to a nice meal that she and Ryder whipped up—minute steak with barbeque butter sauce.

"So, turnabouts fair play," Laney sings. "I think you guys should have us over. I'm dying to see your new place."

"Don't expect much," I'm quick to say.

"He's being silly." Izzy touches her shoulder to mine. "There are a lot of crazy cats and lots and lots of love. You're both welcome. I'll even break out the pots and pans—see what I can come up with."

"Can't wait." Laney gives a dreamy sigh to her sister. It's nice having Laney and Ryder as family. I can definitely get used to this. "And, now, if you don't mind, Holt, I think it's a perfect time to share your special treat."

Izzy turns to me. "Were we in charge of dessert?"

"No, but it's sort of a sweet treat. Laney, why don't you do the honors."

"Brace yourself, Izzy." Laney bounces in her seat as if she's about to burst. "You and I are the new owners of the Electric Lights Dance Studio!" She leans in. "I want to help you with this, Iz. This is technically your baby. But I don't want you to feel burdened or overwhelmed. I'll pick up the slack however you need me to." She holds out her hand. "Congratulations, partner. You're half owner of the ELDS."

Izzy leans back in her seat as if she needs the support. Her features bleach out. She's holding her breath, clearly stunned by the news.

"No kidding?" She looks to me for a moment.

"No kidding. Congratulations, Iz. I know you can turn those dance shoes into gold." I lean in and steal a kiss right here at the table.

Things have finally turned around for us.

We're headed in the right direction. We faced the demons of our past and turned our relationship into gold.

Nothing can stop us now.

But there's still one more demon I need to slay.

ೞೞಚ

While the girls celebrate with copious amounts of champagne and chick flicks, Ryder makes an excuse about needing to meet with a potential client downtown for a quick drink, and we take off.

"Quick drink, huh?"

"Chuck Dupree owns a pawnshop right next to a liquor store. Sounds like just the right excuse we needed."

"How about I buy you a drink after? I have a feeling we're going to earn it."

"Deal. And, by the way, I know we always haven't gotten along, but I'm glad you're with Izzy. You make her happy."

"When haven't we gotten along?" I'm fucking with him because I know exactly what he's talking about.

"When you dated Laney. It pissed the shit out of me. How would you like it if I dated Iz?"

"Got it." I settle back in my seat as we trade cityscape for countryside outside the window. "Yeah, that must have sucked for you." Hell, I knew it did. "But, for the record, she asked me to do it. She thought it would drive you insane. Worked, didn't it?"

"Sure did." He nods toward the black highway. We drive a good forty-five minutes before pulling into a rundown strip mall with nothing but a pawnshop and liquor store. A nail salon is boarded up at the far end. "So, this is where he's holed up. He runs the place with his nephew. I called and said I was interested in a few things—spoke to him myself. He said he'd be here until ten if I wanted to stop by and chat."

"Good work." I crack my knuckles. "I think it's time to have that chat." We get out of the car and head inside. It's dark, smells like piss with the faint scent of an artificial deodorizer that's long since expired.

Two men huddle over an array of colorful bottles—both tall with the same dull scowl on their face, but the one on the left is old as dirt, so I assume it's him. His eyes slice right through me, dark and barren much like his soul I'm guessing.

"You Chuck Dupree?" I cut right to the chase.

"The one and only." He tilts his head as if I were boring him to tears.

"You remember a girl by the name of Izzy Sawyer?"

"Elizabeth?" His brows arch straight into his forehead because this son of a bitch just figured out which direction this is headed in.

I lunge for him, pulling him across the counter until his boozed-up breath is raining down on my face. He's thick and heavy, and I want to gouge out his sorry eyes when I think of where he put those crooked hands.

"She's the one. Consider this a gift from her." I pull him over and start pummeling my fist into him hard and fast. My knuckles dig into his flesh—into his jawbone until I feel it pop beneath me. He lets out grunt after grunt without putting any real effort into fighting back. Before I know it, the nephew and Ryder are getting into it. Ryder goes flying out the door, and I catch a pair of dirty Levis stomping over through my peripheral vision.

I pull back just in time to see a bright blue vase hovering over my head.

Shit.

This is going to hurt.

☙◗◙

My eyes feel as though they've been glued shut. My head feels as if it's wrapped in bricks, and my mouth won't open on command. All I manage to do is get a few weak moans out.

"Holt?" A familiar voice shrills over me in a panic. "Holt, baby, come back to me. Come on, cowboy—we've got a hell of a lot of rodeos to get to."

A dull laugh rattles through me.

Izzy. I try to open my eyes, but my lids won't crack.

"You can do it!" Her sweet voice strings out the words like a song. "I'm right here. Just smile or look at me. I just need to know that you're okay—that you're going to be able to give me some more of those sweet whiskey kisses."

"Iz." I manage to push the words out of the iron trap that my mouth has become. My eyelids split, and the world warbles in and out like a blur.

"Holt! Oh my, gosh, I love you! I love you so much, please wake up for me."

I take a deep breath and force my eyes open, then I see her. Her hair is pulled back. She looks frightened and happy all at once. The room comes into focus, unfamiliar with a small TV up near the ceiling.

It all comes back to me, the drive down to the country, the pawnshop, the man with the vase.

Crap. At least I made it out alive—mostly.

"Ryder?" I try to sit up, and my head explodes as if an anvil just fell on it.

"He's fine." Izzy leans in and blesses me with her cool, soft lips. "You'll be fine, too. The doctor says it's nothing more than a concussion. Be thankful."

My neck knots up and I wince. "Do you know what happened?"

"You sent good old Chuck a thank you note from me. He was going to press charges, but Laney and I had a little talk with him. I wouldn't be surprised if he wrote *you* a thank you note right back." She gives a little wink. "Thank you for that. But please, don't ever go vigilante on me again."

"You were worth it. Sorry I didn't kill him."

"Don't be. I'm over it. I filed a formal complaint with the police so they know what went on, and, if possible, he'll be added to the predatory watch list. Laney said she'll come with me to speak to a lawyer and see what options I might have. He apologized through tears until we left."

"He should have done it sooner."

"I didn't need his apology. Thanks to you, I've moved on. But I need you alive and well to do that, so no more mortal combat. Deal?"

"Deal."

Izzy climbs into the bed next to me, and we hold each other like that all night long.

We did it.

Izzy and I crawled through hell and came out the other side. We're survivors, and we did what we know best—survived.

She lands a kiss on my lips, and I hold her there just like that.

Her heart thumps over mine, and I drift off to sleep, just feeling the love—just breathing Izzy, one heartbeat at a time.

14

Wishes and Dreams

Izzy

One week later

The Black Bear Saloon is roaring tonight. It's the final round of the epic search for house bands, and Laney, Baya, Roxy, and I have migrated to the far end of the bar in a meager attempt to save our sanity.

"So what do you think?" Laney's eyes elongate as she sticks her finger down her throat.

"The first band was definitely the best." Baya nods with such exuberance I almost think she means it. They sounded like shit, though. But that's the nice thing about Baya, she always seems to find the silver lining. I'm glad Laney has someone like Baya in her life.

"Ryder says there's a wild card tonight." Roxy looks over her shoulder at her brother. "He and Holt went scouting off campus and found a garage band to shake up the votes."

"Nice," I say. Holt vaguely mentioned something about it. Strange that he didn't go into detail. We've been inseparable lately. "You never know who can swoop in last minute and steal the win." Sort of the way Holt swooped in and won my heart. I don't know if I'd call it the last minute, but for sure my sanity was beginning to fray in all sorts of unflattering directions.

Holt pops up from behind and lands a kiss on top of my head. "Can I get you girls something to drink?"

Roxy holds up a finger. "Pink Panty Dropper."

"Buttery Nipple." Baya shrugs as she says it.

"Between the Sheets." Laney winks over at Ryder as he and Bryson head over.

"And you?" Holt kneels down beside me. His eyes glow in this dim light. His smile is dazzling and electric.

"A strawberry daiquiri. Make it a vir—make it whiskey." I lean into this beautiful man who is all mine from head to toe. "Make it anyway you like it."

His lids hood low. That lewd smile dips into his cheeks, and my panties want to slide off voluntarily.

Holy hotness, I'll never get over the fact that Holt Edwards is a god that has come down to live among us.

"Make mine whiskey, too," Roxy is the first to abandon her sexed up drink.

"Me, too." Baya pushes her shoulder into Laney.

"Me three." My sister is quick to cave.

"What's up?" Bryson asks as the boys join us.

"It's about to rain whiskey," I say, and I have no idea why. Obviously Holt is much better at persuading people to purchase hard liquor than I would have guessed. If he keeps this superpower up, the bar has the potential to double its take in a month.

The microphone squeals as Cole introduces the next band in the lineup.

"Let's hear it for the wild card pick of the evening, *Twelve Deadly Sins!*" The crowd whoops it up as if it were the second coming of the Beatles. "Let's get some thunder going on up here!" Cole incites the bar into a riotous howl. The tables, the floor vibrates as a thousand coeds harness the ability to split the atom by way of stomping their stilettos.

Cole comes back and joins us just as one of the waitresses brings a rectangular bottle filled with our own brand of liquid gold—whiskey. Holt sits next to me and wraps his arm around my waist. It's been a week since the incident, and he's healing nicely, just a few stitches up by his forehead that have yet to be removed.

Bryson pours us each a shot.

"Let's toast." Bryson nods over to me, and we all lift our glasses. "To Izzy and Holt. Make it last forever."

"*Forever.*" We each touch our glasses to one another until it sounds as if a xylophone is filling the air with its crisp, clear hum.

Holt leans in and brushes my cheek with a kiss.

"Why are they toasting us?" I whisper.

"Because they know I'm about to do this."

Holt drops to one knee, and a tiny jar appears in his hand. Painted on the side it reads *Wishes and Dreams.*

He unscrews the lid, and I'm momentarily blinded by the glittering rock inside.

"Elizabeth Sawyer, would you do me the honor and make all of my wishes and dreams come true? Would you be my wife?"

I take in a breath and clap my hand over my mouth. Holt is proposing. Holt wants to spend the rest of his life with me. All of the faces staring my way melt into the background, the music fades—the room feels as if it's slipping away into another dimension, and it's just Holt and me sharing this intimate moment.

The music shifts to a slow song, and the lights dim as the coeds scream with approval.

"How about it, Iz?" His cheek slides up one side just the way I like it, and my insides melt. "You in?"

"Yes, *God* yes." I fall over him, tangling myself up in Holt and this beautiful love we share. Holt slips the ring on my finger and blesses it with a kiss.

The lyrics start, and I hear my name.

Izzy, the first time I saw you—I knew it was you for me right from the beginning...

"Holt, they said my name."

"I know they did, kitten." Holt pulls me up. "I asked them to. I found these guys last week, and they worked with me until we nailed it. This song is for you, Iz. I helped write it." He buries a scorching kiss onto my lips.

"*Holt!* You didn't have to do that." My cheeks flush with heat. "But I'm glad you did."

"They're playing our song"—he nods toward the dance floor—"shall we?"

"By all means." I can't believe this gorgeous man is going to be my husband. I can't believe this wild card of a band is singing a song that sounds as if the lyrics were ripped straight from my soul. Mostly, I can't believe any of this is my life.

Holt leads us to the dance floor, right into the heart of the crowd as a sea of coeds look on.

"You're incredible, you know that?" I say as we wrap our arms around one another and sway to the music just like we did that first night we kissed.

"It's just a reflection of who you are. You ready to do this life thing with me?"

"I don't think I can do it any other way."

The band sings, *Just give me some more of your whiskey kisses, I can't get enough of those whiskey kisses, and when the night comes to an end and we're holding each other tight, I whisper—you in, and you say…"*

"All the way, baby." I whisper directly into Holt's ear as the band finishes the song.

Holt pulls back and gives the hint of his bone-melting grin. He crashes his lips to mine, and the bar, all of Hollow Brook fades away.

Oh, yeah.

I'm all in.

*Thank you for reading **Whiskey Kisses** (3:AM Kisses #4). If you enjoyed this book please consider leaving a review at your point of purchase.

Look for **Rock Candy Kisses** (3:AM Kisses #5) Annie's story coming soon!

Acknowledgments

Big thank you to all of my wonderful readers that have enjoyed and supported the 3:AM Kisses series from the beginning. It was such a pleasure giving you Holt and Izzy's story. I hope you've had fun with the previous adventures at Whitney Briggs University, and I look forward to sharing more with you. Big hugs to all! I love you guys!

To my spectacular proofreaders and betas, Christina Kendler, Rachel Tsoumbakos, Kathryn Jacoby, Rachel Dick, Delphina Miyares, words cannot express enough how grateful I am to you! Christina Kendler, you have no idea how blessed I feel to have you take time out of your insanely busy life to do the things you do for me. I'm deeply indebted and thankful for all of your hard work. Rachel Tsoumbakos, you are an Aussie rock star and a word ninja of the highest order! I am so humbled to know you. Kathryn Jacoby, boy am I ever glad we met! You are an angel. Your keen eyes are like no other. A million words couldn't express how thankful I am for you. Rachel Dick, I have such mad love for you girl! I know you are so busy with your own life and that makes me that much more thankful that you would read for me. Huge thank you for that. Delphina Miyares! You truly are a super reader and a super person. Your input has saved me countless times. Thank you to the moon and back for lending me your beautiful mind. I cannot wait to go to dinner with you again. This must happen.

To Sarah Freese, my saving grace, who puts up with far more than she ever should. How do I thank you for the countless hours and late night interruptions that I've put you through? Thank you for always having the answer. I heart you like crazy, girl.

Finally, to Him who sits on the throne; worthy is the Lamb. Your word is manna for my hungry soul. For Yours is the kingdom, the power, and the glory forever. You alone are enough. I owe you everything.

About the Author

Addison Moore is a *New York Times*, *USA Today*, and *Wall Street Journal* bestselling author who writes contemporary and paranormal romance. Her work has been featured in *Cosmopolitan* magazine. Previously she worked for nearly a decade as a therapist on a locked psychiatric unit. She resides with her husband, four wonderful children, and two dogs on the West Coast where she eats too much chocolate and stays up way too late. When she's not writing, she's reading.

Feel free to visit her blog at:

http://addisonmoorewrites.blogspot.com
Facebook: Addison Moore Author
Twitter: @AddisonMoore
Instagram: http://instagram.com/authoraddisonmoore

CPSIA information can be obtained at www.ICGtesting.com
Printed in the USA
LVOW12s1952030216

473521LV00009B/771/P